THE RAPTUROUS KISS

"I LOVE YOU!" he said. "I love you until it is impossible to think of anything else but you. I cannot live without you!"

Then his lips were on hers.

To Mina it was as if there was a blazing light which came from the sky and enveloped them with a beauty that was also part of their hearts and souls.

It was so rapturous, so utterly and completely glorious that for a moment she felt as if she must have died and found Heaven, where she and the Marquis were alone except for the glory of God himself.

Winged Magic

Barbara Cartland

Winged Magic

First Published in United States 1981
© 1981 Barbara Cartland
This Edition Published by Book Essentials South 1999
Distributed by BMI, Ivyland, PA 18974
PRINTED IN THE UNITED STATES OF AMERICA
ISBN 1-57723-429-4

Author's Note

The study of birds has intrigued and puzzled Ornithologists for centuries. No-one really knows why some travel three thousand miles in almost unbroken flight, while the partridge and the pheasant do not move more than three miles from the place they were born.

March in England sees one of the most remarkable mass movements of birds. The great rook roosts, where there are nightly gatherings of thousands, break up after the winter. The foreign rooks go overseas to Scandinavia and Germany, while the native rooks start nest-building.

The tiny wren is a migrant who stays until the autumn, then flys to the South of France and Spain, crosses the Mediterranean, and, by some navigational knowledge of its own, crosses the Sahara and penetrates deep into the continent of Africa.

Swallows leave this country in September and arrive eventually in the small Kraal in Africa from which they set out seven or eight months later.

What gives them a fantastic sense of aerial navigation unknown to Cabot, unthought of by De Gama?

Winged Magic

Chapter One

1882

"Mina, you must help me!"

The door opened and a girl came rushing into the small bedroom.

For the moment she was too intent on what she was saying to notice the behaviour of the girl to whom she was speaking.

Then when she saw that Mina was weeping, she said in a tone of consternation:

"What is the matter? What has upset you? It is so unlike you to cry."

She ran across the room and put her arms round her friend, who was seated on the bed with her hands up to her face.

"Tell me what is wrong. I have never seen you like this before."

Christine Lydford's voice revealed her concern, and her dark eyes were soft with compassion.

Very pretty, with her dark, curly hair and white skin, Christine missed being beautiful, but she had a fascinating look of mischievousness about her expression which enchanted most people who saw her.

With a dimple on each side of her mouth, she always seemed to be laughing, and she was undoubtedly the most popular girl in Mrs. Fontwell's Seminary for Young Ladies.

Mina, to whom she was speaking, made an effort to control her tears, then taking her hands from her face she said in a tragic tone:

1

"My ... father is ... dead!"

"Oh, Mina, I am so sorry!" Christine exclaimed. "But how has he died, and where?"

"I have had a letter from my Uncle Osbert," Mina replied, "to say that Papa ... caught something called ... 'Sand-Fly Fever.' He ran a very high temperature, there was no qualified Doctor in that part of Egypt, and he died before my uncle could reach him."

"I am so sorry."

Christine knew as she spoke what a blow this would be to her friend, for Mina's mother had died a year earlier.

Mina had told her that her father was so miserable and lost without his wife that he had gone off to Africa to study the wild life and in particular the birds, because as a hobby he was an Ornithologist.

Mina therefore had been sent to School.

Someone had told Sir Ian Shaldon that Mrs. Fontwell's was the best, and he had therefore sent his daughter to Ascot, where the School was situated, to await his return.

Mina had at first been lonely and afraid of the other girls.

She had lived a very quiet life with her father and mother in the wilds of Huntingdonshire and had never spent much time with companions of her own age.

She had therefore been grateful when Christine Lydford was kind to her, and they had soon become close friends.

Actually, Christine was nearly a year younger than Mina, but no-one would have guessed it, for in appearance Mina looked little more than a child.

Christine, owing to the fact that not only was her father, Lord Lydford, extremely rich but she was an heiress herself, having been left money by her grandmother, had a sophistication which Mina certainly lacked.

The other girls at the School had at first been

amused at what they thought was Christine's patronage of a new girl, then had been surprised when they became inseparable friends.

It was undoubtedly Christine who led, while Mina followed, but they were nick-named "The Inseparables" and there was no doubt that Christine protected Mina from a great deal of subtle bullying.

Mrs. Fontwell's Seminary was very different from any other School.

To begin with, she only accepted pupils who came from the Nobility, and while her fees were exorbitant, she certainly gave good value as regards luxury, if nothing else.

The pupils who could afford it were allowed to bring their own lady's-maids with them, have their own horses in the stables, and take so many extra lessons that their bills increased term by term.

Nevertheless, there was a waiting-list and Mrs. Fontwell's unusual methods of education which made her the envy of other Schools certainly paid off.

Mina, as Christine sometimes said teasingly, had only been accepted "by the skin of her teeth" because her father was no more than a Baronet, and as her bedroom was one of the smallest in the School, it was obvious that the fees Mrs. Fontwell received from her were on the lowest scale.

Christine, on the other hand, had not only a large bedroom with two windows overlooking the garden but a Sitting-Room attached to it.

Her lady's-maid turned her out looking so elegant that most days she might have been attending a Garden-Party at Buckingham Palace, rather than sitting in the class-room.

Mrs. Fontwell saw to it that even the class-rooms were different.

Some of them were Sitting-Rooms in which the pupils when they were studying poetry or literature sat round in armchairs, and there were no desks to give a scholastic appearance.

3

One of the most important rooms in the School was the Ball-Room, where twice weekly the girls received dancing-lessons from experienced teachers.

This of course was an "extra," as were fencing, swimming, Badminton, music, and art.

In fact, Mina, who could afford very few extras, often wondered what exactly was included in the basic fee.

Now with a worried expression in her gentian-blue eyes and her lashes wet with tears she said to Christine:

"It is not only that Papa is ... dead which is making me so ... unhappy ... there is ... something else."

"What is it?" Christine asked.

"I have had a letter from my uncle, and so has Mrs. Fontwell, saying that as Papa was in ... debt when he ... died, I have to find myself some ... form of ... employment."

Christine looked at her in astonishment.

"You mean you have to work?"

Mina nodded. Then the tears came again as she sobbed:

"Mrs. Fontwell has a ... suggestion as to what I should do ... but I cannot bear it ... and yet I suppose I shall have to ... accept."

"To do what?" Christine asked.

She could hardly believe what she had heard, for it was inconceivable that any of the girls at the School should ever have to work for their living or indeed be anything but wealthy.

Because at the moment it was impossible for Mina to speak, Christine merely tightened her arms round her and said:

"I am sure it is not as bad as you think it is. Tell me exactly what has happened."

With an effort that somehow seemed pathetically brave, Mina wiped her tears away and after a moment said:

"My Uncle Osbert, who is the Colonel of his

4

Regiment, says that now that Papa is . . . dead and has left no . . . son, our house belongs to . . . him and he intends to . . . shut it up."

"Why should he do that?" Christine asked angrily.

"He is not married and is always with his Regiment, and of course, as he says in his letter, I could not live there . . . alone."

"It sounds to me a rather high-handed if not brutal way of behaving," Christine remarked. "Go on!"

"He then said that he would settle Papa's . . . debts, but all he could give me was an . . . allowance of fifty pounds a year until I . . . married, when I would . . . receive nothing."

Christine made an inarticulate sound of disgust but did not interrupt, and Mina went on in a small, rather frightened voice:

"He then said I must find . . . employment of some . . . kind, and in his letter to Mrs. Fontwell he suggested that perhaps I could teach . . . children."

"And what did 'The Dragon' say to that?" Christine asked.

"She said I could stay here and teach the younger girls painting and music, and also look after their rooms."

Christine stiffened.

"You mean wait on them as a maid?"

"I think that is what she . . . intends," Mina replied, "because she said she has wanted for some time to dismiss Miss Smith, and if I looked after the rooms it would save the . . . wages of a . . . house-maid."

"I have never heard of anything so disgraceful!" Christine cried angrily. "You are quite right, Mina. You could not bear it. We all know how she treats Miss Smith!"

As she spoke, both girls were thinking of the very junior mistress who was always in trouble with Mrs. Fontwell and trembled in front of her employer like a frightened rabbit.

5

Everything Miss Smith did was wrong, and she was snubbed, scolded, and found fault with until all the girls in the School were sorry for her.

At the same time, as they were also frightened of Mrs. Fontwell, whom they called "The Dragon," no-one was brave enough to stand up for her.

Christine was well aware that if Mina took Miss Smith's place, she too would be reduced to a frightened, trembling wreck.

"It is something you certainly cannot do!" she said positively. "And you will have to tell The Dragon so before she sacks Smithy."

"That is another thing that is ... upsetting," Mina said in a low voice. "I asked Miss Smith a little while ago why she did not ... leave, and she said she was an orphan and had ... nowhere to go to. She was certain that if she did try to find another position, Mrs. Fontwell would not give her a reference."

"That woman is a tyrant!" Christine said. "Though poor Smithy has to put up with her, you certainly will not stay here in such conditions."

"What else ... can I do?" Mina asked in a frightened voice.

"You will come with me!"

Mina looked puzzled and Christine said:

"That is what I have come to tell you. I am leaving!"

"Now? At once?" Mina asked in a puzzled tone. "But the term has only just started."

"Yes, I know," Christine agreed, "but if you have had a disturbing letter, so have I."

Mina gave a little cry.

"I have been so selfish in talking only about myself! Tell me what has upset you."

"It is not exactly upsetting," Christine answered, "but I did come to ask for your help. However, although mine is a difficult problem, yours is far worse, and I intend to solve it for you."

Mina gave her a watery little smile.

"You are so kind. But of course I must not . . . impose on . . . you."

"You would never do that," Christine said, "but let me tell you first why I am leaving."

Mina wiped her eyes again almost fiercely with her handkerchief. Then as Christine took her arm from her, she turned sideways on the bed so that the two girls were facing each other.

Christine drew in her breath as if what she had to say was very momentous. Then she began:

"I have had a letter from my Stepmother saying that Papa has been appointed Governor of Madras, and she has to leave immediately to join him in India."

"I am so glad about your father!" Mina exclaimed. "I am sure it is a very important position, and you must be very proud."

"I would have been more pleased if he had taken me out to India with him as I wanted him to a year ago," Christine replied. "But now it is too late. I have plans of my own."

Mina looked puzzled, then her friend gave a little laugh.

"Not that being in India would have been as amusing as it sounds. My Stepmother would have seen to that!"

Mina knew how Christine hated her Stepmother and was convinced that since she married Lord Lydford she had done everything to prevent him from being as fond of his only child as he would have been otherwise.

"As you know," Christine went on, "when Papa first went to India, he was travelling about the country on a special mission for the Viceroy, and he thought that owing to the heat it would be too tiring for Stepmama. Now she is going to 'Lord it' as a Governor's wife, and she will put up with a great deal of discomfort for that!"

She spoke somewhat spitefully in a voice which

Mina hated, and instinctively she put her hand on her friend's arm to say:

"Go on telling me what has . . . happened."

Christine smiled.

"I know you dislike my ranting on about Stepmama, but wait until you hear the whole story."

"That is what I want you to tell me."

"Because she is going to India, Stepmama has made arrangements that I should leave here."

"Leave?" Mina ejaculated in horror.

She thought that, having lost her father, if she had now to lose her only close friend, her life in the future would not only be lonely but empty.

"She informs me," Christine went on, "that I am to go and live, properly chaperoned, of course, with the Marquis of Ventnor."

"But why?" Mina asked. "Is he a relation?"

Christine gave a scornful laugh.

"Not legally. He is in fact Stepmama's latest Beau!"

For a moment Mina thought she must have misunderstood what Christine was implying. Then she said:

"I . . . I do not . . . understand."

"I am not surprised, and I would not have understood either if I had not realised what was going on between Stepmama and the Marquis, and if Hannah had not found out what they intended for me."

Hannah was, as Mina knew, Christine's lady's-maid.

She had been with her ever since she was a baby, was still more of a Nanny than a maid, and she adored Christine, round whom her whole life centered.

"Why should the Marquis want you to live with him?" Mina asked.

"Stepmama's explanation," Christine answered, "is that since there would be difficulties about arrangements in the holidays while she is so far away, she would feel so much happier if I were under the

8

same roof as somebody she both respected and trusted."

Christine's voice was tinged with sarcasm as she went on:

"A friend who would see that I did not become acquainted with any unsuitable people, while at the same time I had a chance to enjoy myself in the way my father would wish."

"It sounds as if she was really being considerate," Mina murmured.

"Considerate?" Christine exclaimed. "That is how it may appear on the surface! Of course everybody will think it is an excellent arrangement because the Marquis has a number of desirable residences and, according to Stepmama, elderly relatives who would be delighted to chaperone me until she and Papa return to England."

"Perhaps you will enjoy . . . yourself."

"That is not the real reason for all this 'consideration,'" Christine cried. "My Stepmother intends me to marry the Marquis!"

"But . . . you said he was your Stepmother's . . . Beau."

"He is. She has been having a passionate love-affair with him since Christmas."

"I cannot . . . believe it!" Mina said in a shocked voice.

Because she had always lived very quietly with her father and mother in the country, she had had no idea of the immoral behaviour of many of the ladies and gentlemen in High Society until Christine had told her about them.

Then she was quite certain that her friend was exaggerating as she often did.

How was it possible that ladies who moved in Court Circles could be unfaithful to their husbands, or a gentleman be prepared to make love to a friend's wife?

When Christine related these scandalous stories

to Mina, they had sounded so wild and far-fetched that she thought they were merely inventions of her fertile imagination.

Now she said in a firm little voice:

"I am sure, dearest, you are mistaken, and if the Marquis wants to marry you he could not possibly be ... in love with your Stepmother, and anyway you are too young to be married."

"I shall be seventeen in two months' time," Christine said, "and then I intend to be married!"

"To the ... Marquis?"

"No. To somebody quite different! I have not yet told you about him."

Mina's eyes opened so wide that they seemed to fill her whole face.

"Christine! Can you really mean what you are saying?"

"I intended to tell you," Christine said, "but Harry was very insistent that it was to be our secret and nobody else's, so I swore to him I would not breathe a word to anyone."

"Then perhaps you should not tell me now."

"I have to tell you," Christine said. "Harry will understand, but first let me finish about the Marquis."

She saw that Mina was listening intently and went on:

"The Marquis has the reputation of being the most dashing and raffish man in the whole of London. He has had affairs with dozens of beautiful women. I have heard people gossipping about him for years."

"Do they really say such ... things in ... front of ... you?" Mina asked.

Christine smiled.

"No, of course not. They treat me as a child."

"Then how do you know?"

"Because, dearest Mina, servants always gossip to each other as if the children were stone deaf, and servants know everything!"

She thought her friend looked shocked, and she went on quickly:

"What is more, when at home I have my own ways of finding out what is going on."

She smiled before she added:

"I know you will disapprove, and that is why I have not told you before, but there are quite a number of places in our house, which is very old, where one can hear what is happening in the next room."

"You mean you have ... eavesdropped?" Mina asked.

"It is what generations of Lydfords must have done before me," Christine said defensively. "I would not have done it when Mama was alive, but where Stepmama is concerned it is different."

Again her voice had sharpened as she spoke of her Stepmother, and Mina gave a little sigh as she said:

"Go on with your story."

"My Stepmother has been infatuated with the Marquis ever since Papa left for India. Usually she has stayed away at other people's houses, where she met him, or he had parties at Vent Royal, which is his house in Hertfordshire, but when he stayed with us there was no doubt what they felt about each other."

Christine was silent for a moment, then she said passionately:

"It made me sick to hear them kissing in the rooms which had belonged to my mother, and while Papa was away in India."

There was no doubt that Christine was upset, and Mina slipped her hand into hers to say:

"I am ... sorry it has ... upset you, dearest."

"Some of the things they said I did not understand," Christina went on. "Once or twice I heard my name mentioned, but it was just casually, and I did not think it particularly significant."

"And yet you say ... now you are to ... marry him?"

"It was Hannah who told me what my Stepmother had been plotting when her letter arrived this morning. You know I have no secrets from Hannah."

Mina nodded.

"I told her that my Stepmother had arranged for me to go and stay with the Marquis," Christine continued, "and Hannah exclaimed: 'It's true then what Miss Parsons tells me last holidays, an' I thought she was making it up just to tease me!'"

"What was she planning?" Mina asked.

"That if Stepmama had to leave for India, I should go and live with the Marquis and that afterwards, when I was older, he would marry me."

"Why should she want you to do that?"

"See how she has worked it out!" Christine answered. "If he wants a young, complacent, unsuspecting wife, what could be better than a girl of sixteen who he thinks knows nothing of the world?"

Christine drew in her breath as she went on:

"Hannah said Miss Parsons, who is Stepmama's lady's-maid, told her that the Marquis has always said to his close friends that he would never marry a woman who was likely to be unfaithful in the same way as his lady-friends were."

"You mean he thinks it is wrong?" Mina asked.

"Only for his wife," Christine answered scornfully. "He is quite prepared for other men's wives to behave badly with him, and as Papa sometimes says: 'There is no-one more respectable than the poacher turned game-keeper.'"

Mina did not smile. She was only looking worried.

"I still cannot...understand why the Marquis should choose you."

"He has not chosen me," Christine replied. "Stepmama has done that! Do you not understand that she thinks if he marries me she will be able to see as much of him as she wants, and they will be able to continue their affair when she comes back from India. I assure you, she has no wish to lose the Marquis."

"But it is ... wrong and ... horrible!" Mina exclaimed.

"Of course it is!" Christine agreed. "And that is why I am going to marry Harry. He really loves me, and he has done so for three years."

"Marry ... Harry?" Mina exclaimed. "But who is he?"

"He is the Earl of Hawkstone's second son," Christine answered. "He has told me that although I was only fifteen he fell in love with me the moment he saw me, but he knew I was far too young and he would have to wait until I was older."

"Did he tell you that he loved you?" Mina asked.

Christine's eyes were shining.

"He did not say so then, but I knew he thought I was attractive, and when we met when I was out riding I fell in love with him."

"But you were very young."

Christine smiled.

"Sometimes I think I have never been young like you, and certainly not as ignorant or as innocent as you are, Mina."

"To me you have always seemed very sophisticated and grown-up," Mina agreed, "but I thought that was because I had met so very few people and am very inexperienced."

"When I fell in love with Harry I grew up overnight," Christine said simply. "Of course at first we had to keep it a secret because Mama would not have agreed, but he often came to the house and we saw each other."

She smiled tenderly and went on:

"Although he said very little, I knew that he mattered to me in a way I cannot explain, but which made him different from every other man."

Mina knew that ever since Christine was twelve there had been men who found her attractive and had tried to kiss her.

They had written to her what to all intents and purposes were love-letters, but those she had kept she

13

had made Christine tear up in case Mrs. Fontwell should find them.

She had never heard her speak before with such a serious note in her voice, and she said almost reproachfully:

"You have never told me this."

"At first I was afraid that it might be unlucky," Christine replied. "Then after Mama died, when Harry came to the house Stepmama would not even let me see him, so we met in the woods and he told me that he intended to marry me."

There was a rapturous note in Christine's voice as she went on:

"I knew then that I loved him and would never love anyone else in the same way."

"But you are so young!" Mina objected.

"Many girls have been married at seventeen, and Harry said we must wait until my birthday, and then he would ask Papa."

"Do you think your father will agree?"

There was just a little pause before Christine said:

"Harry's father may be an Earl, but as he is only a second son, I am afraid that because I am so rich, Papa, and certainly Stepmama, will say I could do better."

She spoke scornfully, then she added:

"That is why I am running away."

Mina gave a cry of protest.

"Running . . . away?"

"Harry and I are going to Rome, where Papa's younger brother lives," Christine explained. "He married an Italian girl of whom the family do not approve. That is why I am certain that in Papa's absence he will constitute himself my Guardian and give permission for Harry and me to be married. He will do so partly to spite the family and partly as a champion of romance."

"It does indeed sound very, very romantic!" Mina said. "But are you sure you are doing the right thing?"

"Quite, quite sure," Christine said confidently. "I love Harry and he loves me, and we are prepared to wait until I am seventeen. But I know that if the Marquis proposes to me, which he intends to do, Papa and Stepmama will make me marry him!"

"Are you quite certain he wants to marry you?"

"Quite certain!" Christine said. "According to Hannah, he has always had this idea of finding a young, innocent, untouched wife who would not interfere in his rakish pursuit of other women, and now Stepmama has done all the hard work for him and produced me like a rabbit out of a hat!"

She sounded frightened as she continued:

"Once I get to Vent Royal, you know as well as I do that I shall be trapped, and that is why first thing this morning I sent a telegram to Harry and he met me in the shrubbery after luncheon."

"How could he do that?" Mina cried.

"Quite easily, and it is something I have done before," Christine answered. "As you know, The Dragon has a rest at two o'clock and we are all supposed to do the same. I merely slipped out the side-door and kept in the shadow of the trees. When I reached the shrubbery, Harry was waiting just inside the gates!"

Her face was suddenly radiant as she said:

"He loves me! He loves me so much, Mina, that he agreed we could not risk losing each other, and we will leave for Rome as soon as I reach London."

"And when will you do that?"

"We leave tomorrow!"

Christine clasped her hands together.

"Harry is so clever. He saw at once that if Papa's carriage arrived on Thursday, as Stepmama said in the letter, it might be difficult to get away when I reach London, where the Marquis's horses will be waiting for me."

"Then what have you planned?" Mina enquired.

"He has sent a telegram, signed with the name of Papa's secretary in London, saying that the plans have

15

been changed and the carriage will come for me tomorrow."

As if she thought Mina could hardly follow what was arranged, she said:

"But of course the carriage that arrives here will not be Papa's but one that Harry has hired. I shall then drive not to our house in Grosvenor Square, but to Hawkstone House. Harry's father is not in London, and from there we will set off for Rome first thing in the morning."

"It sounds very complicated to me," Mina said. "You are quite certain you will not be caught?"

"If I am, there will be a terrible row both for me and for Harry," Christine said. "And because Mrs. Fontwell may insist on someone chaperoning me to London, I was going to ask you to come with me."

"But of course I will do anything..." Mina began.

She was silenced by a sudden cry that was almost a scream from Christine.

"Mina! I have an idea! A brilliant idea!" she said. "But wait a minute—let me think about it."

She put her fingers to both her temples as if at an effort to concentrate. Then she said slowly:

"You will come with me to London, but we will tell The Dragon that you are doing so because I have engaged you as my companion."

Mina's eyes widened but she didn't speak, and Christine went on:

"It is something I am only too willing to do, dearest, and I promise that whatever happens, you shall never stay here and work in such a degrading position. But let me go on ...".

She closed her eyes to think more clearly before she said:

"Instead of returning here to School after I have left with Harry, you will go to Vent Royal and stay with the Marquis until I am married."

"What are you ... saying ... what do you ... mean?" Mina asked.

"You must see," Christine said. "It makes everything much safer for me and gives you somewhere to live until I can send for you."

"Are you saying...that I...should pretend... to be you?"

"It is quite easy," Christine replied. "He has never seen me!"

"Never...seen you?"

"No. Stepmama saw to that! She never allowed any women near him if she could help it, and when he came to dinner when Papa was there, all the women guests were either old or ugly."

There was almost a sneer on Christine's face as she said:

"The only reason why she is letting me near him now is because I am the better of two evils. Either he will find somebody to take her place—beautiful, attractive, and fascinating, as apparently all his women are—or else he will find some stupid and innocent wife over whom Stepmama will have no control."

"I understand what you are...saying," Mina said, "but honestly, dearest...I could...not take your...place. For one thing...he would know at once I was not...you."

"Why should he?" Christine argued. "I tell you, he has never seen me. I was always told to stay in the School-Room, but I used to watch him through the many peep-holes in the house and think how much I disliked his outrageous behaviour."

Her voice was angry as she went on:

"As I have told you before, to make quite certain I never interfered with Stepmama's arrangements in the holidays, she always provided me with a 'Warder' in the shape of an ancient, retired Governess who was quite harmless and a bore."

Christine sighed.

"If I had not sometimes stayed with my cousins in Devonshire and Mama's relatives in Edinburgh, I think at times I would have gone mad!"

"You had fun with them?"

17

"Lots of fun, thank goodness, which Stepmama did not know about, or she would certainly have stopped me from going to them," Christine replied. "She dislikes me as much as I dislike her, and she has always resented me because Papa is so fond of me."

Mina said nothing.

Once again she thought that Christine was exaggerating what she had suffered from her Stepmother. At the same time, she was extremely shocked at what Christine had told her.

How could any woman of the importance of Lady Lydford behave in such a fashion? And certainly the Marquis sounded an exceedingly undesirable person with whom she had no wish to become acquainted.

As if she sensed her hesitation, Christine said:

"Dearest, dearest Mina, please help me. If you will not do this, I may very likely be prevented from marrying Harry, for you know as well as I do how many things could go wrong on the long journey to Rome."

"How can you travel with him alone?" Mina asked.

"It is perfectly proper if Hannah is with me," Christine explained. "If anyone is the personification of propriety and morality, it is Hannah, as you well know."

Mina laughed as if she could not help it. It was certainly true.

Hannah, who was a strict Presbyterian, watched over Christine with eyes as sharp as a hawk's. Nothing that was in the least reprehensible would occur while she was in charge.

"I admit that Hannah will be a very efficient Chaperone," she said at last.

"Too efficient, if you ask me!" Christine replied. "But she likes Harry, and that, you must admit, is a very strong point in his favour."

"How old is he?"

"He is just twenty-seven, ten years older than I, and therefore very capable of looking after me once I am his wife."

Christine gave a rapturous little sigh.

"Oh, Mina, I love him so much, and I am so happy, so very, very happy! I thought this year would never pass because I wanted so much to be with him. But now, if my uncle agrees, we shall be married at once, or we may have to go into hiding where no-one can find us until I am seventeen."

As she spoke, Christine reached out to take hold of Mina's hands.

"That is where the danger lies, you can see that. So please, please, Mina, say you will help me. I cannot lose him, and my whole life's happiness depends on him."

"I . . . I am afraid I shall . . . fail you."

"You will not do that, and you will play the part better than I ever could."

"The part?"

"Of a young, innocent girl, not quite seventeen."

"But I am a year older than you."

"Well, you certainly do not look it."

Christine gave a little laugh as she added:

"Of one thing I am quite sure: no-one would employ you as a teacher except The Dragon, who would be getting you cheap."

Mina sighed.

"That is something I thought myself."

"In fact, if you ask me," Christine said, "you look about fourteen, and that, I am quite certain, will please the wicked Marquis!"

"I am sure he will not believe I am you. Perhaps he has seen a photograph of you, or a painting."

Christine laughed.

"The only photographs that have ever been taken of me were taken at home and they all make me look as if I were coming out of a fog, and were not focused properly, or whatever the word is, and I have never been painted."

"But my clothes are not as elegant as yours are," Mina said weakly.

"That is certainly a point," Christine said. "Your

19

clothes are very pretty, but anyone as experienced in women's dress as the Marquis will be aware that they are not expensive."

She paused before she exclaimed:

"I have it! You remember those clothes that grew too tight for me and were, I thought, far too young?"

"I think I ... remember ... them."

"Well, last year, both in the summer holidays and at Christmas, I bought a whole new wardrobe," Christine said, "and Hannah packed all my old things into a trunk. We would have taken them home at Easter but there was no room in the carriage, so I left them here. As far as I know, they are still up in the attics."

There was just a flicker of interest in Mina's eyes, for Christine, being so rich, always wore the most exquisite and expensive clothes that were the envy of every girl in the School.

When her mother was alive she had taken her to all the best Bond Street shops, and while her Stepmother complained that it was a quite unnecessary extravagance, she had continued to order her clothes from the same places.

Not all the girls at Mrs. Fontwell's School came from rich families, but there was a great deal of competition among them, and a number of the older ones tried to rival Christine in appearance.

But she had an exquisite figure and extremely good taste, so she was always the undoubted winner of the contest and remained the unrivalled Queen of the School in her Bond Street gowns.

Christine rose from the bed.

"I will go and tell Hannah to get the servants to bring down that trunk," she said. "If I had not been so selfish, I might have thought of giving them to you at the time."

"I have been quite content with my own gowns," Mina replied, "and perhaps yours will not fit me."

"They will, I am sure they will," Christine said. "I have grown a lot this last year, but you appear to have remained the same size."

She suddenly put her arms round Mina.

"You want somebody to look after you, dearest," she said, "someone like Harry. I promise you, when you join us after we are married I will find you a charming and delightful husband."

"All that matters," Mina said, "is that you should be happy, and quite frankly, Christine, I do not want to be married. I think it would be very frightening, unless I was very much in love."

"When you are, you will find it is not frightening but marvellous!" Christine said.

She walked towards the door, saying:

"Get packed while I go and tell The Dragon I am taking you with me. You can be assured she will then reverse her plan to dismiss the wretched Smithy. She has to have somebody to torment."

As Christine said the last word, the door shut behind her, and Mina shuddered.

She was well aware that if she had been in Miss Smith's place she would indeed have been tormented, and it would have been an humiliation to know that the other girls pitied her because she had ceased to be a pupil and had become a mere employee to be ordered about and abused as Mrs. Fontwell thought fit.

'Anything would be better than that,' she thought.

Then she was afraid.

How could she possibly pretend to be Christine? How could she go to stay with the Marquis of Ventnor and not be exposed the very moment she arrived?

And if she were, it would be a very unpleasant position to be in.

Could she really believe that any man could be so cold-blooded as to choose a wife because she was too young and too stupid to be aware of his behaviour with other women?

Could Lady Lydford be as improper and as scheming as Christine averred?

Mina knew that Christine often exaggerated both her likes and her dislikes.

21

At the same time, she had never been untruthful to her personally, and she could imagine no reason why she should invent such a story.

Mina was also horrified at the idea that Christine could run away to be married without her father's permission, but then Lord Lydford was very unlike what her own father had been.

At the thought that she would never see him again, the tears welled up in Mina's eyes.

Although she had been very close to her mother, she had loved her father, first as a child, then as a girl idolises the first important man in her life.

Somehow, in some strange way which she could not explain to herself, Mina had felt when he set off to travel abroad that she had lost him.

It was then that she had cried herself to sleep night after night because she had a presentiment that he would never return.

"Papa! Papa!" she sobbed. "Do not leave me. Please, please come back!"

Because she knew he could not hear, she prayed fervently every night that he would be safe and nothing would prevent him from coming home.

But her prayers had not been heard, and now her father was dead and so was her mother.

The only close member of her family was her Uncle Osbert, whom she had not seen for years and who had always seemed to disparage her father for not becoming a soldier.

But her father had not wanted to kill anyone, and she knew that his gentleness was the reason why he had a strange power over animals.

Dogs and horses would follow him wherever he led them, and once he had tamed a wild otter so that the animal trusted him and would come when he was called.

But birds were her father's specialty. He had taught Mina about their habits and she had loved him to tell her tales of species which were almost extinct and which could be found only in far-off places in the world.

Now she wished, as she had wished a thousand times, that she had been with him as she had wanted to be. Perhaps she would have been able to save him when he was ill.

The tears ran down her cheeks as she thought of him suffering while his native servants did not know how to help him.

"Papa! Papa!" she cried. "If only I could come to you now and ask your advice!"

She tried to think of what he would say if she told him of Christine's plan.

Then she was sure of one thing: he would hate her to be in the same predicament as Miss Smith.

Mrs. Fontwell was unmitigatedly cruel to the young Governess, and her father had hated cruelty.

What was more, he had often said that to humiliate a human being mentally was as wrong as injuring them physically.

"Our minds are very sensitive, Mina," he had said once, "and are the expression of our souls and our hearts. Always remember that what we think today, we become tomorrow."

She had been very young when he had said that, and she had not quite understood at the time. But as she grew older she had come to realise that a person's thoughts can influence their actions, and actions, good or bad, begin in the mind.

As she wiped away her tears, Mina thought that her father would tell her, if he were beside her, which perhaps he was, that she must solve this problem for herself not emotionally but with her brain.

She thought for a moment, and she felt she could almost see her father wandering along the coast of Africa, curious and excited and finding it all an adventure.

"That is what Christine's plan for me is," she decided, "an adventure which I should ... not ... refuse."

Chapter Two

The Marquis of Ventnor, riding back across the fields, realised he had made a mistake.

Previously he had always avoided being amorously involved with any of his neighbours, knowing that when the affair was over, which in his case was usually a short time, it was uncomfortable to meet the lady concerned on County occasions.

But Lady Bartlett had been very persistent in her pursuit of him, and as Lord Bartlett was frequently in attendance on the Prince of Wales, they met continually in London.

Very alluring with dark hair and slanting green eyes that promised exotic delights even when she was speaking of the most banal and commonplace things, Lady Bartlett had succeeded in strongly attracting the Marquis, but only after she had made him aware that he was the most exciting man she had ever met.

Eloise Bartlett had a way of talking to a man as if he were the one person she had always wanted to meet and what he said to her was as enticing as the song of Solomon.

Because the Marquis and Lord Bartlett sat together on many Hertfordshire Committees and were frequently involved in dealing with agricultural difficulties, he did his best to prevent himself from being caught in the net which Lady Bartlett spread for him.

He was well aware that it was a net, and he knew as much about her reputation as she knew about his.

In fact, it was not surprising that Lady Bartlett had evoked the disapproval of the Queen, for although Her Majesty spent much time at Windsor, she was extremely well informed as to what was happening in the Social World.

She was especially suspicious, resentful, and positively antagonistic to those who were friendly with her son and whom she considered to be a bad influence.

Lady Bartlett undoubtedly came into the last category.

The Prince had for a short while been obviously infatuated with her, and the gossip must have reached Windsor quicker than any carrier-pigeon could have conveyed it.

When the Prince transferred his affections, Lady Bartlett looked quickly round for another lover.

He would have to be distinguished, otherwise she would have lost face amongst her contemporaries who were already triumphant in knowing that she had lost the Heir to the Throne.

She had kept him interested for a while, but his affection had waned even more quickly than she had anticipated, leaving her conscious that her position must be rectified.

The Prince of Wales was undoubtedly the greatest prize that the Social World could offer to any woman.

But not far behind him came the Marquis of Ventnor.

There were of course several Dukes on the social scale in between, but the Marquis went unrivalled in respect of wealth and reputation.

He had also just finished a liaison with a very attractive widow who might have lasted longer had she not been so obviously intent on marrying him.

The Marquis's marriage was a subject of bets in White's and a great number of other Clubs.

Time after time it had seemed to his contemporaries that he was on the brink of becoming "leg-shackled," whether he liked it or not, but always by some instinct for self-preservation he had managed to escape at the eleventh hour.

The widow, however, had somewhat foolishly not only over-played her hand in public, but had told him in private at a very intimate moment how desperately she wished to belong to him "for eternity."

The mere word was enough to make the Marquis shudder.

Every woman with whom he was involved bored him sooner or later, and he was well aware that it was due to a fault in his character which he could not rectify.

He often asked himself why.

Some of the women by whom he had been fascinated were not only alluringly passionate but also intelligent.

They certainly had the type of sharp wit that made him laugh, and they would not have been included in the Prince of Wales's intimate circle had they not been able to add to the amusement of their friends by being entertaining as well as beautiful.

The Marquis had often asked himself what love really was and why he would suddenly realise, usually at a most inconvenient moment, that a woman could no longer make his heart beat faster and that he had no more desire to kiss her or even to touch her again.

That was what had happened this afternoon, and he said to himself as his horse trotted over the green fields which joined Lord Bartlett's Estate with his:

"I have been a fool!"

He had met Eloise in the Summer-House which was situated in the shrubbery of the garden which surrounded Lord Bartlett's stately home, and it was a place they had often used before.

It was furnished with soft rugs on the floor and a comfortable couch with silk cushions, and because

Eloise was experienced in the need to cosset and pamper a man, there was always a bottle of the best champagne open in a silver wine-cooler.

When the Marquis reached the Summer-House just before five o'clock, Eloise had been waiting for him with outstretched arms and red lips raised enticingly to his.

It flashed through his mind that she was too impetuous and it would have been more effective if she had left him to make the first overtures and had greeted him less effusively.

Then the fire in her eyes and on her lips had aroused an answering flame in the Marquis, and it was only later, when having drunk a glass of champagne and said that he must leave, that there was any ordinary conversation between them.

"Must you go so soon?" Eloise Bartlett had protested, pouting provocatively at him as she spoke.

"I have things to see to at home," the Marquis answered evasively.

"What sort of things? I thought you were alone at Vent Royal."

"I am, except for my grandmother."

"Fortunately she is an old woman," Eloise replied, "otherwise I should be jealous."

The Marquis did not reply. He merely set his glass down and picked up his high hat and riding-whip.

Eloise, lying back on the couch and looking, as she well knew, very beautiful with her flushed cheeks and slightly dishevelled hair, threw out her arms.

"Come and say good-bye," she suggested softly.

The Marquis shook his head.

"I have been caught that way before, Eloise," he said. "Instead I will thank you for making me very happy."

He had put his hand on the door when Eloise gave a little scream.

"When shall I see you again? Can you come tomorrow or the next day?"

27

"I will send you a message in the usual way," he answered. "I may be going back to London—I am not sure."

"To London? But you have only just come to the country and you told me that you intended to stay for a week."

There was no doubt that there was a note of reproach in Lady Bartlett's voice.

The Marquis knew that as she disliked the country, the only reason why she had accompanied her husband when he decided to attend the High Sheriff's Garden-Party was that he had said that he also intended to be there.

"I will let you know when I can come again," he said.

He walked out of the Summer-House, and he heard Lady Bartlett's voice still protesting as he moved through the shrubs to where he had left his horse.

As he rode off, he knew with that strange feeling of finality which had come to him before on far too many occasions that he would not go back.

He could not explain why, but quite suddenly and unexpectedly Eloise Bartlett no longer interested him.

He was aware that when she had asked him to say good-bye and he had replied that he had been caught that way before, it was the all-too-familiar story.

A woman's desire to go on love-making when the peak of passion was past, and to entice a man who was ready to leave to stay just for a little longer, inevitably brought about a repetition of what had already occurred.

'It is like hearing the same tune over and over again,' the Marquis thought, 'until it exasperates one.'

Once again he acknowledged that he had made a mistake in being involved with the wife of his neighbour.

At first it had been rather intriguing to agree to

Eloise's suggestion that they should meet in the Summer-House.

It was so cleverly contrived that he realised that he was not the first man to have used that particular rendezvous.

Yet, because he found her fascinating, that did not worry him any more than he minded that her servants who arranged the silk cushions and the champagne were well aware that she was meeting somebody surreptitiously.

Nor did he ever consider that his own servants must be curious as to why he went riding late in the afternoon or, as on several other occasions, at night after dinner.

It was no use for the Marquis to hope that none of them would talk, for he was quite certain they would do so, and there would be another story to add to those already circulating about him and his numerous affairs.

What he found depressing was the problem that awaited him at Vent Royal, which had started with a letter that had arrived the day before from Lady Lydford.

Lady Lydford had actually, although she was not aware of it, begun to bore him nearly a month ago, and because of his feelings for her he had returned to Eloise Bartlett, who had appeared on his horizon only a short while before Easter.

His affair with Nadine Lydford had lasted longer than most of his liaisons.

At Christmas they had stayed in a Ducal house-party which the Marquis had found more amusing than any party he had attended for years.

He decided that a large part of the attraction had been the fact that Lady Lydford, whom he had met only two months previously, had been there and he had found her not only beautiful but amusing.

What she said was invariably spiteful and witty at someone else's expense. At the same time, her sharp tongue stimulated him in the art of repartee, and they attracted jointly an admiring audience in the rest of the party.

The food had been delectable and the wines superb, and, because the weather was comparatively mild, the hunting on the Duke's horses had been excellent.

There were several shoots at which the Marquis proved himself such a crack-shot that he achieved a record bag, and at the Balls in the evenings Lady Lydford glittered with diamonds and shone like the proverbial star.

Because her husband was abroad, the Marquis had no need to feel irritatingly secretive in his approach to her, and they were automatically paired together at meal-times and at the card-tables.

When they returned to London, their desire for each other mounted higher and higher, and because their friends were only too willing to entertain them, they went from house-party to house-party or she was included among the guests at Vent Royal.

Sometimes there were large parties when the Prince of Wales was the principal guest. Sometimes there were smaller ones at which it was easy for him to be alone with Nadine Lydford and to enjoy her ability to make him laugh.

Then inevitably, so insidiously that he was hardly aware of it, the flames she had ignited began to flicker and cool down.

Unlike Lady Bartlett and a number of his other loves, Nadine Lydford was far too clever to suggest that they should love each other for eternity or to make it obvious that she was twining herself about him, determined to keep him enslaved by her attractions.

He had revealed to her the idea which had been in his mind for a long time.

It was that when he married, as his relatives had begged him to do for years, it would be to a woman who would be faithful to him and be a model wife in the old-fashioned meaning of the word.

Lady Lydford was sure that like so many other men he was enamoured of the idea of being married to somebody like the Queen.

She had loved Prince Albert to distraction, and when he died she had mourned him so excessively that she had retired from public life to live alone at Windsor Castle.

Personally, Lady Lydford had thought it the most ridiculous thing she could imagine any woman doing.

But she was well aware that the Queen when she was a young girl had evoked the protective instinct in everybody who served her, starting with the handsome, attractive Lord Melbourne, who almost worshipped her.

Then in her widowhood she had made all her Courtiers and Statesmen think that no man could be paid a greater compliment than that his wife should miss him so desperately that no worldly interests could replace him in her life.

"What the Marquis wants," Lady Lydford told herself, "is a young 'Queen Victoria,' babbling that she must be 'good' and looking at him adoringly like some stupid spaniel."

It was when Lord Lydford wrote from India that he had been summoned to Simla to see the Viceroy, who he thought was going to offer him a Governorship, that she knew what she must do.

To keep the Marquis, which was something she fully intended, she must provide him with his "little-girl wife" who would keep him occupied until her return to England.

The opening of the Suez Canal had enormously shortened the voyage to India.

In fact, the journey took only seventeen days, and, having installed herself as the Governor's wife, Lady Lydford was determined to come home for a short visit, during which time she was certain she could persuade the Marquis to return with her.

He had often been abroad, and she suspected that, apart from the example of Queen Victoria, he had also thought the idea of a wife being in *purdah* was from a man's point of view a very convenient one.

Women could be shut up until one wanted them and be unable to interfere with their husband's other interests, whatever they might be.

The more she thought about it, the more Lady Lydford was determined that she would bind the Marquis to her in a way no woman had ever been able to do before.

What could be better than that she should provide him with the wife he needed, and it should be somebody from her own family?

Nadine Lydford was an extremely vain woman, which was, to do her justice, not surprising.

Her beauty had been acclaimed since she had grown from a rather gawky young girl into what her admirers described as a Goddess of Beauty.

She was tall and stately, as was the fashion, carried her head proudly and imperiously on a swan-like neck, and when she entered a room she seemed to sweep all before her like a tidal-wave.

She had been determined to capture Lord Lydford ever since she had learnt that he was not only a widower and therefore free to marry but also extremely rich.

Nadine had been married from the School-Room to a man much older than herself, and once she had tasted the heady quality of applause, she had realised that she was extremely unhappy.

Fortunately, this had not lasted long, for her husband had died.

Then she had been free to indulge in innumerable discreet and certainly amusing love-affairs while she looked for another husband.

Lord Lydford had seemed an ideal match until she realised that if she had waited a little longer she might have married the Marquis.

This thought was so bitter that at times she found

herself forgetting the advantages her marriage had brought her and that she had been wild with triumph when Lord Lydford had finally proposed.

Now her scheming, astute mind was concerned both with keeping her husband happy, especially when he held the important post of Governor, and also with retaining the affection of the Marquis.

"I can do it! I know I can do it!" Nadine Lydford said to herself a dozen times before she left England.

On her last passionate night with the Marquis, she had been too clever to ask if he would go on loving her or to suggest that he might be faithful.

She merely looked wistfully unhappy at the thought that she must leave him, and offered him as if it were a parting present the idea that he should marry her Stepdaughter.

"Christine is everything you want, dearest Tian," she said. "She is young, innocent of the world, idealistic, and—attractive."

There was a sharp note in the last word, as if Lady Lydford found it difficult to say.

Then she added quickly:

"Of course it is of no interest to you, but she is also immensely rich, having been left a fortune by her grandmother, besides the fact that my husband has settled money on her which she can spend when she comes of age or marries."

"There is no hurry for me to find this paragon who, as you are well aware, is merely a pipe-dream," the Marquis replied.

"That is not true," Nadine Lydford said softly. "You know that all your relatives are praying that you will be married and have an heir. Otherwise, if you have an accident out hunting or are shot by some jealous husband, the title will go to that boring cousin who is over fifty."

She felt as if the Marquis metaphorically shrugged his shoulders, and she went on insistently:

"Darling, how could you bear it, or rather how

could we bear it to see him in your place? Of course you must marry and have a son, in fact dozens of them to keep your wife well occupied."

The Marquis laughed a little ruefully.

"I wonder why I was stupid enough to tell you what was in my mind! You are putting pressure on me, and in a way I do not like!"

"If you do not do it now, it is something you will have to do eventually," Nadine Lydford replied. "Then the girl you seek might not be available, and I promise you Christine is exactly what you require."

She thought as she spoke that Christine was not exactly like a young Queen Victoria either in looks or in character, but at least she was pretty, annoyingly so, and quite intelligent.

As the Marquis thought about it, Nadine Lydford looked at him and thought, as she had done so often before, that he was the most attractive man she could possibly imagine.

Not only was he good-looking but there was something aloof and a little detached about him, so that she could never be quite certain what he was thinking or feeling.

Added to his looks were his possessions and his position. The sum total was breathtaking, and she could not and would not lose him.

The Marquis had left with the idea that she had planted in his mind, but once he was away from Nadine Lydford he told himself he had no intention of agreeing to her suggestion.

When they were talking about marriage, he had only rather vaguely told her what he wanted in his wife, simply because he was tired of his relations pleading with him to be married when all he wanted was to be free.

He had confided in Nadine after she had told him that the Duchess of Wrexingham was determined to capture him for her eldest daughter.

"I am well aware of that!" the Marquis snapped. "I wish to God women would leave me alone. If I have to be married, it will be in my own time."

"And when will that be?" Nadine Lydford asked.

"When I find a young, innocent, pure, and complacent wife," he replied.

At the time, he had meant merely to surprise her, but she was shrewd enough to listen in a way which had made him elaborate on the idea.

"Darling Tian, you are so clever to think of anything so original," she enthused. "Of course that is the perfect solution for any man in your position, but few would think of it."

Flattered, the Marquis had elaborated on his theme, really spelling it out to himself rather than to the woman he held in his arms.

Now, confronted with a *fait accompli*, he told himself it was too soon, and anyway he was quite certain the whole idea was impractical.

Then to his consternation Nadine had sent him a letter by hand the following day, telling him that she would send Christine to him while she was away in India so that he could see her for himself.

She added that it would also be a kindness in that she would not have to worry about the child's holidays or the finishing touches to her education, which were so important the last year before she made her début.

> *She will learn so much with you at Vent Royal*, she wrote, *and I know your dear mother, who loves having young people round her, will enjoy having Christine in the house.*
>
> *If she does not come up to your high expectations, then the moment I return I will make other arrangements. But I feel you will find her the ideal wife for whom you have been searching, and there will be no need to look further.*

Nadine had finished her letter with some flattering and clever compliments which the Marquis found amusing, as well as an effusive tribute to his distinction as a perfect lover such as he had heard so often before.

It was only when he had finished reading the letter that he was aware that Christine would have already made arrangements to leave her School.

As Lady Lydford had made clear, all he had to do was to send his carriage to London the following day to collect her from Lydford House where she would be waiting.

'Dammit all! It is an imposition!' he thought at first.

Then as he realised that to untangle such a plan would be quite complicated, he told himself that the mere fact that the girl was coming to Vent Royal committed him to nothing.

People might think it strange that he was having a girl to stay, but she would be very well chaperoned by his mother, and after all, at sixteen they could hardly ascribe her visit as anything more than a kindness to Lady Lydford, who had doubtless found it difficult to take her with her to India.

As the day wore on he began to think that in fact it might be rather interesting.

As Lady Lydford had sensed, the Queen's devotion to her husband had seemed to him both touching and admirable. And also, when he was in the East she had considered that the Maharajahs' custom of keeping their wives in *purdah* was, from a man's point of view, an ideal arrangement.

What he was not prepared to admit even to himself—in fact he would have thought he was being hypocritical if he had—was that deep in his heart he was shocked by the immorality of the Society women with whom he spent his time.

He was intelligent enough to know that the Prince of Wales's attitude which had set a new fashion was a direct reaction against the prudery of the Queen's Court, itself a reaction against the excesses of the Prince Regent who was afterwards George IV.

At that time, the licentiousness of the Bucks and Beaux had been a scandal.

But the solemnity of Prince Albert had been boring in the extreme, and the Marquis had often laughed at the early Victorians who had even draped the legs of pianos and tables in case they might arouse immoral desires.

Now it was accepted in the Marlborough House Set, in which the Prince of Wales reigned supreme, that once a beautiful woman had married and had presented her husband with several children including the all-important son and heir, she could indulge in discreet *affaires de coeur* as long as there was no open scandal.

What was going on was of course no secret to her intimate friends, and doubtless she discussed her admirers with them, counting each one as a feather in her cap.

The Marquis had seen complacent husbands sitting, as was expected of them, in their Clubs from four o'clock in the afternoon until it was time to go home and dress for dinner, and had told himself it was something he never intended to do.

It was, in his opinion, degrading.

It was one thing to be the ardent lover, the man who captured a woman's heart and made her his, whoever she belonged to legally; but it was quite another thing to be cuckolded and humiliated by knowing one's wife preferred another and doubtless better man.

"It is something I could never endure!" the Marquis said.

Although he allowed himself to be pursued, captivated, and fascinated by the beautiful women who desired him, he was aware that what he felt for them was entirely physical and that some part of his mind and perhaps his soul was shocked by their permissiveness.

Occupied in these thoughts, the Marquis had been riding over his own broad acres and now he was in sight of Vent Royal.

It was a beautiful house, very different from Lord Bartlett's and in fact from every other mansion in the County.

Vent Royal had been built in the time of Charles II, after the Restoration had given the Royalists back their Estates and when England flourished after the privations of the Commonwealth.

The newly crowned King had started one of his first journeys round the country by staying at Vent House and had then changed the name to "Vent Royal."

Succeeding generations of the Vent family had added to the building, making it very much larger and in the last century very much more impressive.

Yet it still retained something of the magic it had when it was first built.

It always seemed to the Marquis that the laughter and elation of the King who had waited so long for his throne echoed in the older part of the house where Charles had slept and doubtless enjoyed himself with one of his alluring mistresses.

The Marquis had instinctively from the time he was a boy modelled himself on the King, perhaps because portraits of Charles II hung in so many of the rooms and the atmosphere he had left behind never seemed to be erased.

He had read every book obtainable about Charles II, admiring his wit, his wisdom, and his determination to keep physically fit.

He followed the King's example by riding, swimming, sailing, racing, and playing tennis.

Charles had once when talking to Lord Clarendon referred to his daily game of tennis as his "usual physic," and the Marquis thought that perhaps making love came into the same category.

It was of course inevitable that the other side of the King's character, which included a desire for lovely women and the enjoyment he had found in their company, should make the Marquis wish to emulate him in that as in everything else.

He sometimes thought wryly that there were just as many Barbara Castlemaines, Nell Gwynns, and Louise de Keroualles in his life as there had been in the King's.

Charles had taken a pure, virginal maid for his wife, and it was unfortunate that she had not been able to provide him with the heir he needed so badly.

In this respect also the Marquis intended to follow King Charles's example.

The sun was sinking and the brilliant colours in the sky were reflected in the hundreds of windows at Vent Royal.

They glowed warm, golden, and welcoming, and the Marquis felt as if they reached out towards him, asking for his love and his promise to serve the ideals for which Vent Royal had always stood, as his ancestors had served them in the past.

He suddenly felt that it was not only his duty but a sacred trust that he should give the house and his great Estate an heir who would carry on the many reforms and modern ideas that he himself had initiated since he came into the title.

Only a few people knew how progressive the Marquis was as a land-owner and that despite his frivolous reputation he was deeply concerned with the conditions in which those who served him lived and the well-being of those who resided on his Estates.

Only his private secretary was aware of how generous he had been to hundreds if not thousands of people who turned to him for assistance.

As he looked at his house, perhaps for the first time the Marquis admitted that it was time he married.

'I shall be thirty-two next birthday,' he thought. 'If I grow too old I shall not be able to teach my sons to shoot and ride, or squire my daughter to her first Ball.'

His lips twisted a little wryly at the thought of being a *pater familias*.

Then he knew it was not only his duty but perhaps would be a new interest in his life to prevent him from becoming so quickly bored with the women who at first had seemed so desirable.

He had finished with Eloise Bartlett, and he knew if he was honest that he had no wish to see Nadine Lydford again.

He was glad she had gone to India, but she had certainly left a memory of herself behind her in the shape of her Stepdaughter.

'Today! She arrives today!' the Marquis thought.

It was extremely irritating that everything had been arranged in such haste, and he was well aware that Nadine had acted as she had simply to prevent him from refusing to accept the girl.

In her letter she had not even bothered to tell him the name of the School from which she was coming, but had made sure that he would have to collect her because otherwise she would arrive in London and just wait for his carriage.

"Dammit! She has been extremely high-handed!" the Marquis said furiously.

Then he laughed.

He had always appreciated the shrewdness of Nadine Lydford's mind, which enabled her to get what she wanted, while she cloaked an iron determination with honeyed words and sweet lips.

It was a sort of ruthlessness the Marquis thought he had himself, and as he was not deceived he found it difficult not to appreciate such methods.

"If the girl is a nuisance," he decided, "I will put her on a ship and send her out to Madras."

If she was sixteen, he reckoned, it would be at least a year before he could marry her, and that gave him plenty of time to find out if his idea of educating his future wife was possible or was merely, as he had said to Nadine, an insubstantial pipe-dream.

However, he was certain now that the whole idea was really ridiculous, and if he was honest he had only produced it as a kind of protection against those who schemed too obviously and too ardently for a wedding-ring.

What was more, he had no experience of young girls.

Various of his Vent relatives had children, but when he thought about them he could not remember their ages.

He was almost certain he had never seen a really attractive young girl among them.

He had the idea, however, that girls of sixteen were rather gawky, like young colts, gauche, uncertain of themselves, and undoubtedly tongue-tied.

"How could I bear that?" he asked, remembering the amusing conversations at the dinner-parties at Marlborough House and Sandringham.

Only to think of the brilliant table-talk or the ladies in their lovely gowns with tiaras on their well-dressed heads, their ear-rings glittering with every movement, made him feel nostalgic.

He thought of the beauty of Princess Alexandra, her classical features and her lovely eyes which looked at the Prince of Wales adoringly despite the fact that his eyes roved in many other directions.

"She is a perfect wife," he told himself, and he was aware that when she came from Denmark she had been very young and unsophisticated.

"That is the right way to be married," the Marquis decided positively.

Then as he rode up the deep gravel sweep to the front door he added with a smile:

"At least what Nadine has arranged for me will be something new and perhaps in its own way an adventure."

* * *

The Marquis on entering the Hall handed over his hat and whip to one of the liveried footmen in attendance.

As he did so, his secretary Mr. Caruthers came towards him.

There was an expression on his face which told the Marquis that, as he had expected, his visitor had arrived, but he waited until his secretary said:

"Miss Lydford is here, M'Lord. She arrived over an hour ago."

The Marquis thought there was just a touch of reproach in his secretary's voice, as if he thought the Marquis should have been there to welcome her.

"I am sure you have seen that she has everything she wants, Caruthers," he replied. "Where is she now?"

"She has changed, M'Lord, from her travelling-clothes and is waiting for Your Lordship in the Library."

The Marquis looked slightly surprised and Mr. Caruthers explained:

"I thought of course of having her shown into the Drawing-Room, but as I was not certain how long Your Lordship would be before your return, I thought the young lady would like to look at the books and of course the newspapers which are always in the Library."

"Quite right, Caruthers," the Marquis approved. "Has Miss Lydford met Her Ladyship?"

"May I remind you, My Lord, that you told me this morning when you were discussing the matter that you would take Miss Lydford up to Her Ladyship yourself."

"Yes, yes, of course. I had forgotten," the Marquis said.

As he spoke he had been walking towards the Library, and now as he neared it he did not say any more. He realised that Mr. Caruthers was with his usual tact leaving him to make the acquaintance of his guest alone.

It suddenly struck him that she might have found it rather frightening to arrive in a strange house, and that if he had had more time to think about it he should have sent somebody to collect her in London.

Somewhere in her letter Lady Lydford had said she would bring a maid with her, and he supposed that would have counted as some sort of companion, so there was no reason really for him to feel guilty.

A footman opened the Library door.

It was a large room and the walls were covered with books from floor to ceiling.

The collection was famous and contained many priceless first editions.

The Marquis was used to people exclaiming at the magnificence of it and also being very impressed by the painted ceiling.

As he entered the room he thought at first it was empty. Then he saw somebody not looking at the books as he had expected, nor reading the newspapers and magazines which lay on the long, low tapestry-covered stool near the fireplace, but instead staring out the window.

It surprised him that Christine was so small, much smaller than he had ever expected.

Then as she must have heard him she turned from the window to look in his direction and thought there must have been some mistake.

The face before him was not that of a young girl as he had expected, but somebody who seemed little more than a child, but very pretty—in fact a lovely child with a small oval face framed with fair curls and large blue eyes that were now staring at him.

The Marquis walked towards her.

Then as he drew nearer he saw to his surprise that the expression in the child's eyes was unmistakably one of fear.

Chapter Three

As the horses carried her nearer to Vent Royal, Mina grew more and more nervous.

She told herself that she should never have agreed to such a frightening arrangement, but she knew that the alternative, which was to stay at School and be subjected to all kinds of humiliation by Mrs. Fontwell, was even more terrifying.

At first it had seemed exciting to run away with Christine, who was in an exalted mood at the idea of meeting Harry.

It was also a consolation for Mina to know that among all the other trunks on the roof of their carriage was one containing the beautiful gowns that Christine had given her, besides hats and bonnets to match them.

She had never imagined that she would ever own even one gown so expensive or so attractive, and strangely enough, although she had been doubtful about it, they fitted her perfectly.

The gowns were of expensive material, but they had a deceptive simplicity about them and Mina kept wishing her father could see her wearing them.

The fashion had dispensed with the large bustle, which now was replaced by a large bow low down on the back of the skirt with cascading lace or caught-up folds of satin.

The tiny waist, the tight bodice, and the small sleeves were exceedingly becoming, and while Christine had grown out of these gowns, they were just the right length on Mina.

Mina was so effusive in her thanks that Christine was rather embarrassed.

"I am so ashamed, dearest Mina," she said, "that I had not thought of giving you the gowns before now. When you come to Italy I promise you shall have a whole trousseau of beautiful clothes."

"Please do not say that ... word," Mina pleaded. "It frightens me!"

"Just as it frightens me," Christine replied, "to think that unless you help me I might be forced to marry the Marquis."

Although she did not say so, Mina thought that Christine was right in judging from his reputation that the Marquis would make any woman unhappy.

She had often wondered what the Rakes whom she had read about in her history-books were like. Now, she thought, she would not only meet one but live in his house.

"I must look on it as an experience," she told herself, trying to be brave, "and not show him that I am ... shocked at his ... behaviour."

All the same, she felt that if he did half the things that Christine credited him with, she would in fact be very shocked and it would be difficult to prevent him from being aware of it.

Travelling to London, Christine had talked all the time of Harry, and Mina knew that because of her promise to him she had bottled up her feelings for so long that now they exploded like a cork coming out of a champagne bottle.

"I love him! I love him!" Christine cried. "We are going to be so ecstatically happy together, and thank goodness I am rich, so we will not have to scrimp and save in a cottage."

It flashed through Mina's mind that perhaps Harry was so keen to marry Christine simply because she was an heiress, but when she met him she knew that this was not true and that he loved Christine for herself.

45

Her father had taught her to have an instinct about people as well as animals and birds, and Mina was at once intuitively aware that Harry was honest and sincere and that his feelings for Christine were true.

He was waiting for them at Hawkstone House, and when Christine sprang out of the carriage the moment the footman opened the door and ran up the steps to greet him, Mina heard him say:

"You have come! I could hardly believe that something would not stop you at the last moment."

"No, I am here," Christine replied, and her voice seemed to vibrate with joy.

Then she remembered that Mina was with her, and when Harry was introduced to her they went into the Drawing-Room.

There was tea waiting for them and as Christine poured it out from an exquisite Georgian silver tea-pot Harry said:

"We are leaving very early tomorrow morning, as I want to catch the Rome Express in Paris late tomorrow night."

His voice softened as he added:

"It is a long journey and I do not wish you to be tired, my darling."

"I shall not be tired with you," Christine said.

They looked at each other and everything else was for the moment forgotten, even the tea-pot in Christine's hand.

Then she came back to reality, and when she explained how Mina had promised to go to Vent Royal in her place, Harry was astonished.

"Do you think that is wise?" he enquired.

"You must see that it makes it much safer for us than we should be otherwise," Christine replied. "There is always the chance that my uncle may be away from Rome, or that he may make difficulties about my being married until I am seventeen. Then, if Stepmama heard I was not at Vent Royal as she has arranged, everybody would be looking for me."

"I see your point," Harry said reflectively.

He was a good-looking man, Mina thought, but not as handsome as Christine thought him to be.

However, his fair hair was brushed back from a high forehead, and he looked the perfect example of a healthy, well-bred Englishman.

"It is very kind of you to do this for us," he said to Mina.

"I am very nervous about it," she confessed, "but I want to help Christine. She has always been so very kind to me."

"As I hope she will be to me," Harry said with a smile.

"Could I be anything else?" Christine asked. "Mina, who is my greatest friend, since her father's death has been left with no money, so I know, dearest, you will understand that when we are married I want her to come to Italy or wherever we may be to stay with us."

As Christine spoke, Mina watched Harry's face, thinking that if he was not pleased at the idea or if there was even a pause before he accepted it, she would not impose herself on them.

But he smiled and said instantly:

"Of course! That would be a very good idea, and I am sure Miss Shaldon will not want to stay here and be involved in the rumpus which our marriage will cause."

"Oh, please, I could not bear that!" Mina cried.

"As soon as it is safe I will send you a telegram," Christine promised. "Then you must make some excuse to leave Vent Royal and join us."

As she finished speaking she gave a little cry.

"But of course, I must leave you some money to pay for your journey!"

"No ... please ... I have some of my own," Mina protested.

"Which has to last you a long time," Christine said, having seen the letter Mina had received from her uncle. "I will write you a cheque, but perhaps it would be wise if you do not cash it until you need the money, otherwise it might be stolen or mislaid."

"I promise you I will be very careful," Mina said, "and if I do join you, I will certainly not get in your way and will try to find myself employment of some sort."

As she spoke, she thought that neither Christine nor Harry would really want her while they were honeymooning together, but those difficulties could be shelved until they were safely married.

As if she sensed what Mina was thinking, Christine said to Harry:

"What is important, as you well know, is that we should be married before Papa and Stepmama can do anything about it."

"You know I want that above everything else," Harry said in a deep voice. "I have already made enquiries and found that the British Embassy in Rome can arrange anything for English people abroad."

Christine gave a smile of happiness.

"Now all we have to do is to persuade Uncle Lionel. Since he is already in disgrace with the family, I feel he will not put any obstacles in our way."

"We will keep our fingers crossed," Harry said.

When tea was finished they went upstairs to see the bedrooms that had been arranged for them and to find that Hannah had unpacked two or three gowns for Mina.

She had of course been forced to leave the School in her own clothes, which, she was well aware, looked exactly what they were, cheap material made up by the village seamstress.

Hannah had now produced a most attractive travelling-gown and cloak which Christine had discarded but which to Mina's eyes looked brand new.

With it went a young girl's hat to be worn a little to the back of the head. With Mina's baby face, it gave the impression of a halo.

"What shall I wear to go out to dinner tonight, Hannah?" Christine asked.

The way she spoke made Hannah ask:

"You're not dining here?"

Christine shook her head.

"No. Mr. Hawk says that because his father and mother are in the country, the Chef is on holiday, so we are all going out to dinner."

"If you asks me, that's taking an unnecessary risk," Hannah said sharply. "Supposing someone sees you?"

"Nobody will see us," Christine said positively, "and I have no intention of wasting a night in London eating nothing but bread and cheese. Besides, it will be a treat for Miss Shaldon."

Despite Hannah's disapproval, Christine insisted on putting on one of her prettiest evening-gowns, and Mina chose one out of what she thought of as "the magic trunk" and in which she looked exceedingly pretty.

They drove off with Harry and he took them to a quiet Restaurant where he had booked a table in an alcove which had curtains which partially hid them from the view of other diners.

"How did you know of this place?" Christine asked, as they sat down at the table and Mina looked round her with delight.

Harry smiled.

"That is not the sort of question you should ask me."

"You mean you have brought your lady-friends here?"

"That is another question to which there is no answer."

Mina wondered apprehensively if Christine would resent what Harry's reply suggested, but she only said:

"I am not concerned with your past, Harry darling, as long as you make certain that I am your future."

"You can be absolutely sure of that," he said, "and if you like, I will give you my solemn word of

49

honour that the only lovely lady I shall ever bring here in the future will be you!"

"That is what I want you to say," Christine replied.

Then once again they were looking into each other's eyes and Mina was forgotten.

The dinner was delicious, but as soon as it was finished Harry took them back to Hawkstone House.

"Another night," he said to Mina, "we will all go to the Theatre, but as I do not want Christine to be tired, I think she should now go to bed and dream of me."

"I think it will be difficult to sleep," Christine said, "knowing that tomorrow we start on our great adventure."

"That is exactly what it will be," Harry said, "and an adventure which I believe, my darling, will last us all our lives."

They smiled at each other, and Mina thought how lucky they were.

They loved each other, and whatever the difficulties they would face them together and nothing else would matter.

"But I am alone," she added to herself, "and I have to rely on myself and nobody else."

She thought the same thing when the next morning Christine kissed her good-bye and she, Harry, and Hannah set off for Victoria Station.

"All you have to do, dearest," Christine said, "is to take the hankney-carriage that Harry has waiting for you and go to Lydford House. The only people there will be the caretakers, who are both very old."

"They will know I am not you," Mina said unhappily.

"There is no reason why it should concern them," Christine replied. "All our servants will have gone to the country, which is the usual procedure when Papa and Stepmama are away."

She saw that Mina was looking worried and added:

"You must just wait until the Marquis's carriage arrives, then be in the Hall and instruct his servants—not ours, since they are very decrepit—to carry out your luggage."

It all sounded very frightening to Mina, but actually it had turned out not as difficult as she had feared.

Lady Lydford had obviously sent a note to the caretakers to expect her Stepdaughter.

Because she disliked Christine, she had not made any arrangements for anyone else to help with the change-over of carriages from the one that had brought her from School to the other that was to take her to Vent Royal.

Although she did not say so to Christine, Mina was frightened that Lord Lydford's secretary might appear at the last moment, or even one of the Lydford relations.

However, when everything had passed off without there being any questions asked, she thought that perhaps Lady Lydford did not wish her husband's relatives to know the plans she had for her Stepdaughter.

Anyway, the caretakers were too old and too uninterested to show any curiosity, and the Marquis's smartly dressed footman managed her trunk and hatbox without any trouble.

When the agitation she felt at getting away was over, she appreciated that the travelling-carriage was very comfortable. The four horses pulling it were fine Thoroughbreds, their silver harness bore the Marquis's crest, and the livery of his servants was very impressive.

She had expected that Vent Royal would be magnificent, but what she had not anticipated was that it would be so lovely.

As she drove down the drive and saw it for the first time, she knew it had a charm as well as a beauty that was like something from a dream.

Although her home had been only a small Manor-

51

House in Lincolnshire, both her father and mother had appreciated beauty wherever they found it, and Mina had grown up to find it in what she saw, what she read, and what she heard.

Now as the horses drew nearer to Vent Royal, she thought that even if this experience was a frightening one, there would be compensations in seeing, if nothing else, the great house that lay ahead of her.

She felt sure that it had a fascinating history, and she remembered her mother telling her that most ancestral houses had Curators who knew not only all the contents but the history of each object they guarded and prized.

"I must find out all about Vent Royal," she decided.

On her arrival she was taken upstairs to the most beautiful bedroom she had ever seen, and she felt as if doors were opening for her to pass into a world different from anything she had ever imagined.

"You've not brought a lady's-maid with you, Miss?" the Housekeeper, in rustling black silk, asked in surprise.

Mina had already anticipated this question and replied:

"I am afraid not. Hannah, my maid, had to leave me at the last moment on a matter which concerned her family."

This, Mina thought, was near to the truth. She had already made up her mind that she would lie as little as possible.

"Never tell a lie if you can help it," her father had said to her once. "You are invariably caught out sooner or later."

Mina was sure that was true, and although she had to act a part, she thought that if she told the truth in all matters except those concerning her identity, she would not fail Christine by having her deception discovered.

"I'll get one of the housemaids to look after you,

Miss," the Housekeeper was saying. "How long d'you think it'll be before your own lady's-maid can join you?"

"I really have no idea," Mina replied, "but I shall be very grateful if you can spare a housemaid to attend to me."

"It'll be no trouble, Miss," the Housekeeper replied.

It was obviously expected that she should change her travelling-gown for something lighter, and she put on a very pretty afternoon-dress of white silk trimmed with lace round the skirt and a sash which echoed the blue of her eyes.

Because there was a maid and the Housekeeper to help her, Mina could not spend too long regarding her reflection in the mirror, which was something she wanted to do.

Although she was aware that the gown designed for Christine made her look very young, she knew it was extremely becoming and she had never before realised that she had such a good figure.

Her waist was tiny, and as she fastened her dress at the back the Housekeeper said:

"You've lost a little weight, Miss, since you bought this. I'll get the seamstress who is resident in the house to take it in for you."

"Thank you."

"Like as not, you'll fill out again living here," the Housekeeper went on. "They always say that Hertfordshire air makes you hungry, and that's certainly true at Vent Royal."

"I am sure that is only one of the many marvels you can offer here!" Mina said, and knew the Housekeeper was pleased by her enthusiasm.

When she was ready she went downstairs and the Butler showed her into the Library, explaining that the newspapers were there and she might like to read them while she waited for His Lordship.

But as soon as she was alone Mina ran to the

window to look out at the gardens sloping down to the lake.

On the other side of the water, golden in the sun, she could see huge oak trees in the Park and beneath them a number of spotted deer.

She thought how thrilled her father would have been to see such a large herd.

He had loved deer and often described to her the stags with high antlers he had seen in Scotland.

"You did not shoot them, Papa?" Mina had asked.

Her father shook his head.

"That is something I could never bear to do," he said. "A stag is such a sensitive animal and I prefer to watch them. Next time I go North, I shall be able to photograph them."

Her father had enthusiastically taken up the recently invented art of photography, and although his first pictures of animals and birds had not been very successful, he had persevered until before he left for Egypt his photographs were to Mina's eyes sensational.

"When you come back you will have to have an Exhibition, Papa," she said.

"Then I hope I get snap-shots of animals which are rare enough to be really interesting," he replied.

Now Mina remembered with a little sob that she would never see the photographs he had taken, and perhaps her uncle, not being interested in such things, would not even bother to bring them home with him.

'Perhaps one day I shall be able to afford a camera of my own,' she thought, looking at the deer.

Then she remembered it was unlikely that she could spend her money on anything but necessities.

From the window she could see not only the deer but also birds flying over the garden and butterflies hovering over the flowers.

They were so lovely that for the moment she was lost in a day-dream, and when she heard the door open behind her she turned round automatically.

Then she felt her heart begin to beat frantically in a frightened manner.

She knew that the man who had come into the room must be the Marquis, but he seemed to swim in front of her eyes. Then as he walked forward her vision cleared.

For a moment there was silence. Then as Mina found it difficult to breathe and impossible to speak, the Marquis said:

"I must apologise for not being here to greet you, but welcome to Vent Royal!"

He held out his hand as he spoke, and somewhat belatedly Mina curtseyed.

As she did so, her fingers touched his and she felt as if there was a strange vibration from them and his hand was firmer and stronger than she had expected.

Then she realised that the Marquis was not in the least what she had anticipated.

Because Christine had said such terrible things about him and she had thought of him as a Rake, she had expected him to look dark, sinister, and debauched.

Instead he was strikingly good-looking, with a fair though slightly sunburnt complexion, his hair was dark but not black, and his eyes were steel-grey.

What was very obvious was that his square chin and his firm mouth bespoke determination, and he had a personality which Mina, feeling very nervous, found overwhelming.

"You have had a good journey?" the Marquis asked as she did not speak.

"Yes . . . thank you."

Mina was almost ashamed that her voice sounded so low and shy.

"I would have sent somebody to meet you in London," the Marquis said, "had I had a little more time to plan such things. But I received your Stepmother's letter only yesterday."

He made it sound a reproach.

"I am . . . sorry," Mina murmured.

55

"What is your name?"

Because his question was a surprise and somewhat abrupt, Mina, without thinking, replied:

"Mina."

Even as she said the word she remembered with horror that she was supposed to be Christine.

"I am ... called Mina at ... School," she said hastily, "because I am so small ... but my real name, by which I am called at home ... is ... Christine."

"Yes, of course," the Marquis said, "I remember now. That was what your Stepmother called you in her letter. But I certainly think 'Mina' suits you better, so perhaps that is the name you should use at Vent Royal."

Mina thought hastily that that would certainly make things easier.

"Well, Mina," the Marquis went on, obviously expecting to her to agree, "I suggest that now I take you up to meet my grandmother. As I am unmarried, she lives here, and she is looking forward to making your acquaintance."

He moved towards the door as he spoke, and Mina followed him.

Beside the Marquis she looked very small, her head coming up only to his shoulder.

The contrast was so evident that she thought it was unlikely he would think her older than the sixteen-year-old girl he expected.

Then as they walked up the grand staircase and on to a wide landing hung with paintings, there was so much to look at that for the moment she forgot her fear of him.

The Marquis walked quickly and obviously had nothing particular to say.

He led the way down several corridors and they reached what Mina was sure was the south side of the house.

As he knocked on a large double door he explained:

"My grandmother has her own Suite of rooms here, where she can, if she wishes, have her personal friends to stay. It is an arrangement which I find advantageous because we each, so to speak, have our own separate households."

As he spoke, he was thinking that he would make it clear to this child from the very beginning that when he entertained his personal friends, she would remain in his grandmother's part of the house.

She certainly could not be included in his parties, which would be most unsuitable for anyone so young.

An elderly maid opened the door and curtseyed when she saw the Marquis.

"Her Ladyship's expecting you, M'Lord," she said. "She heard the young lady had arrived and is waiting to meet her."

"I thought she would be curious, Agnes," the Marquis answered.

He walked past the maid into a large room with three windows overlooking the garden.

It was exquisitely furnished, and sitting by the window in a comfortable armchair with an embroidered Chinese shawl over her knees was a beautiful old lady with white hair.

She looked up as the Marquis entered, and there was no doubt, Mina thought, that she was pleased to see him.

"You are late, you naughty boy!" she exclaimed. "I expect you have a very plausible excuse for keeping your guest waiting, but, as you well know, it was impolite!"

"As I have also kept you waiting, Grandmama," the Marquis replied, "you must forgive me."

He crossed the room, took her hand in his, and kissed it with a grace that Mina thought must be unusual in an Englishman.

Then as she followed him to stand waiting, the Marchioness held out her hand, saying:

"I am delighted you are here, Christine. I much admire your father and I am glad to hear he has such an important post in India."

"It is extremely kind of you to have me to stay, Ma'am," Mina said, making a little curtsey.

"You must thank my grandson, not me," the Marchioness said.

There was a mischievous look in her eyes as she added:

"I have never known him to invite anyone so young to Vent Royal before. I am sure it will be a new experience for him."

The Marquis looked quite unperturbed by what his grandmother was saying and merely replied:

"Miss Lydford tells me she is called Mina because she is so small. The name seems to be appropriate."

"I presume it is short for Wilhelmina," the Marchioness remarked.

"I have always thought Wilhelmina a very prudish sort of name," Mina replied, "and much too much of a mouthful."

As she spoke she realised she was not shy of the Marchioness but only of her grandson.

This was the first coherent sentence she had uttered, and she thought his grey eyes were looking at her critically and felt herself blush.

"I think 'Mina' is charming," the Marchioness said, "so we will call you that. I shall be very interested to hear if you enjoy being here and find it easy to comply with the—educational plans my grandson has for you."

There had been a distinct pause before the word "educational" and again there was that mischievous little twinkle in the Marchioness's eyes.

"Do not frighten Mina, Grandmama," the Marquis said, "or she may fly away from us like your white doves. Wicks tells me there are two missing this morning."

"Two more?" the Marchioness said in exasperation. "How annoying! But they may be nesting somewhere in the woods. I feel sure they will come home when they are hungry."

"I hope so."

Mina was listening intently.

"You have white doves, Ma'am?" she asked. "How lovely! It is something I have always wanted to possess."

"They are turtle doves," the Marchioness replied. "Look out the window and you will see them."

Mina needed no further invitation and ran to the middle window of the room.

It looked out over a different part of the garden from that which she had seen from the Library. Here there was a great lawn enclosed with box-hedges trimmed in strange shapes of topiary, and there were several dove-cots. Perched on them and clustered on the ground were a large number of white doves.

It was such a lovely sight that Mina stared at them entranced before she said:

"They are beautiful! Of course it would be very distressing to lose even one of them. How long have you had them?"

"Nearly ten years," the Marchioness answered. "As you can imagine, we have a lot of new ones every year, which compensate for those which fly away or die."

"Perhaps tomorrow I can see them close-to," Mina said.

"Of course," the Marchioness smiled, "and you look rather like a white dove yourself in that pretty gown."

"I only wish that were true. Papa always said I was like a small inquisitive wren."

As she spoke she realised that once again she was speaking as herself rather than as Christine.

She had an uncomfortable feeling that perhaps the Marquis would know if Lord Lydford was interested in birds or not.

"And what is so particular about the wren that

you should resemble one?" the Marchioness enquired.

Mina smiled.

"She is rather an ordinary little bird," she answered, "except that, surprisingly for anything so tiny, she has quite a powerful voice and sings beautifully all the year round."

"And you sing?" the Marquis asked.

The question made Mina jump. Then she said quickly:

"If I say 'yes' it will sound as if I am boasting, but the wren has very few other talents, except that it seems surprising for so small a bird to lay six to eight eggs."

The Marquis laughed.

"You are certainly being very informative."

"I think what Mina is saying is very interesting," the Marchioness said. "I can see you are fond of birds, my dear, and as I am fond of my doves we shall have at least one thing in common."

"I shall hope so, Ma'am."

The Marchioness looked at her grandson.

"I am going to suggest, Tian," she said, "that Mina remain with me for a little while until it is time for me to go to bed. Then, as there is no-one staying in the house, I think she should have dinner downstairs with you."

She paused but he did not answer, so she went on:

"You must get to know each other, although I am sure when there is a party Mina will understand that, until she is a débutante, she must dine upstairs."

"Yes, of course I understand, Ma'am," Mina said quickly, "and I would much prefer that."

She thought it would be a mistake for her to be seen by any of the Marquis's guests, in case they knew Lord and Lady Lydford. Moreover, after all Christine had said, she had no wish to meet the Society women with whom he behaved so outrageously.

'If his friends all behave like Christine's mother,'

she thought, 'then the less I am involved with them, the better.'

Because she was afraid of him and she thought it would be an ordeal to dine with him alone, she said quickly:

"Perhaps ... His Lordship would ... prefer me to have dinner ... upstairs? I should be quite ... happy to have a tray in my bedroom."

"That would be very inhospitable of me," the Marquis said before his grandmother could speak. "Let me say I am looking forward to learning a great deal more about you, Mina, besides your knowledge of birds."

He then kissed his grandmother's hand as he had done before, and said:

"Good-night, Grandmama. Do not stay up too late gossiping with Mina. You know the Doctors say you are to rest."

"Doctors are a lot of old women!" the Marchioness retorted sharply. "As I have said to them often enough, I shall have plenty of time to rest when I am in the grave."

"Which is too far ahead to be worth considering," the Marquis answered.

He walked from the room and when he had gone Mina felt as if she heaved a sigh of relief.

All the time he was there she had been vividly conscious of him, and she found him not only intimidating but, in some way she could not understand, disturbing.

She was not sure if that was the right word, but the feeling was undoubtedly there.

Then she told herself it was because she was aware that he was thinking of her as his future wife.

She only wished she could tell him that it was something she would never be, and that she was shocked and horrified that any man, least of all somebody like himself, should approach marriage in such a cold-blooded way.

Marriage should happen only when two people loved each other completely, as Christine loved Harry and he loved her.

'I wish I could tell His Lordship how foolish and unpleasant his idea of training me is,' Mina thought.

She strongly disapproved of what he was planning to do, but it was of the utmost importance that he should not suspect that she was an imposter. If he did, he might try to prevent the real Christine from marrying Harry.

Remembering the squareness of the Marquis's chin and the firm line of his lips, she was certain he was capable of doing anything to get his own way.

Thinking of him, she had almost forgotten that his grandmother was sitting there watching her with her shrewd eyes.

"What is upsetting you, child?" she asked.

Mina jumped at the sound of her voice.

"I am sorry, Ma'am," she said. "I must have seemed . . . rude, but I did not . . . mean to . . . be."

"I think you were indulging in what are called 'day-dreams,'" the Marchioness said with a smile, "and I was wondering if you were day-dreaming about my grandson. I am sure you find him handsome."

"I was thinking, Ma'am, that he is obviously somebody who is determined to have his own way, and perhaps that is because all his life he has been spoilt."

Mina spoke without realising that it might sound rude, and as she saw the surprise in the Marchioness's face she said quickly:

"Please forgive me. I should . . . not have said . . . that."

"Of course you should have said it," the Marchioness replied. "You were speaking what you thought was the truth. I assure you, I like the truth, especially where it concerns my grandson."

She raised her eye-brows as she added:

"Most young women eulogise over his looks and charm."

Mina gave her a shy little smile, then said:

"I am not being impertinent when I tell you, Ma'am, that my Nanny always used to say: 'Beauty is only skin-deep and it is your character you have to worry about, not you face.'"

The Marchioness laughed.

"That is certainly something you must say to my grandson, though can I really believe that you are criticising him on such short acquaintance?"

"No ... of course ... not ... Ma'am!"

The Marchioness laughed again.

"I think you are, and I am sure it will be very good for him! It will certainly also be an unusual experience."

Mina thought she had made a mistake in saying what she thought.

"Please ... please ... Ma'am," she began. "I did not mean to say ... anything in the least ... derogatory about His Lordship. But I am afraid sometimes ... things ... slip out without my ... thinking before I ... speak."

"I did the same when I was young," the Marchioness said, "and in consequence I had the reputation of being a dangerous wit."

She saw that Mina was listening wide-eyed and she went on:

"It served its purpose, for, since people were never certain what I would say next, they always listened to me. That is just as flattering, I assure you, as when people simply look."

"I am sure they looked at you, Ma'am," Mina said, "because you must have been very, very beautiful."

"Because we have already established that you speak your mind," the Marchioness answered, "I shall accept that as a genuine compliment."

"I certainly did not wait to think about it," Mina said. "It really did just slip out."

The Marchioness laughed again.

"I can see, Mina," she said, "that like the little wren you are going to sing delightfully at Vent Royal, and I am going to enjoy every note of your song."

Chapter Four

The Marquis, standing with his back to the mantelpiece, sipped a glass of champagne as he waited for Mina.

As he did so, he was thinking of his grandmother's amusement that he would have been left with a young girl on his hands.

"This is something quite new, Tian," she had said when he informed her of Mina's arrival. "In the past, if I remember rightly, your lady-friends have left you their horses, their dogs, quite a number of trunks, pictures, and furniture to take care of, and once, I recall, a parrot!"

The Marquis gave a faint smile but did not interrupt, and she went on:

"But never do I remember anyone depositing one of their children on you. This is certainly an innovation!"

"Nadine Lydford had to leave unexpectedly for India."

"Hardly unexpectedly when we all knew months ago that her husband would be offered a Governorship. But I expect she had her own reasons for not joining him sooner and for leaving Mina with you."

There was no doubt of the innuendo in the Marchioness's voice. But her grandson, who enjoyed her intelligent thinking and even her teasing, merely replied:

"She felt I might be able to give the girl that extra polish which will make her glitter in the Social World in which her Stepmother already shines so brilliantly."

"I am quite certain that if the girl attempted to do any such thing, Nadine Lydford would snuff out a rival light with a heavy hand."

The Marquis laughed as if he could not help it.

He knew his grandmother disliked Lady Lydford and, although she had been too tactful to say so openly, disapproved of their liaison.

He had been half-afraid that because of her feelings for the Stepmother she might take it out on Mina.

But it seemed from the moment of her arrival that Mina's childish charm had delighted the Marchioness, and he thought with satisfaction that the future boded fair.

The door opened and as Mina came into the room the Butler announced:

"Miss Lydford, M'Lord."

As she crossed towards him the Marquis watched her critically, realising that she had none of the awkwardness he would have expected. Indeed, she moved with a grace that might be the result of teaching and with a lack of self-consciousness that was entirely natural.

When she was near enough she curtseyed and he found himself appreciating not only her movement but her gown.

As a connoisseur of a woman's appearance he was aware that it was an expensive garment, while at the same time its almost exaggerated simplicity was in excellent taste.

He wondered if the choice had been Mina's or Nadine Lydford's, and he had the idea that the latter would not have tried very arduously to make her Stepdaughter look so attractive.

"Good-evening, Mina!" he said. "I suppose it would be incorrect to offer you a glass of champagne? But perhaps as this is our first dinner together we might bend the rules on such an auspicious occasion."

"Thank you, My Lord," Mina replied, "but only a very little if you please."

The Marquis fetched a glass of champagne from where it had been left on a side-table and as she took it from him she said:

"If I were to propose a toast I should do so to your house, which is so beautiful that I think it must have emerged right out of a dream."

"I am glad you feel like that," the Marquis replied. "I am very proud of Vent Royal and of being the owner of it for my lifetime."

"In other words a 'Trustee of the Future,' as your ancestors must have been before it passed to you."

The Marquis was surprised that she grasped his point so quickly, but before he could say any more the Butler announced dinner and they walked into the Dining-Room which had been redecorated in the last century.

It was very impressive with pillars at one end, a carved marble mantelpiece, and a particularly fine collection of paintings on the walls.

After they sat down, the Marquis saw Mina looking at them and with a faint smile said:

"I see you are interested in paintings."

"I hope I am interested in everything that is beautiful, and I see you have a very fine collection of Lelys."

"He painted the beauties who embellished the Court of Charles II," the Marquis replied, "and the one opposite you, which is a particularly delightful example of his work, is Barbara Castlemaine, the Duchess of Cleveland."

Mina was looking at the portrait intently and the Marquis said:

"She was certainly very beautiful, and do you not think your Stepmother is also an exceedingly beautiful woman?"

He asked the question out of curiosity, but what he did not expect was that Mina, who had been

looking at the paintings with a wide-eyed interest,
suddenly stiffened.

She had in fact been so much absorbed in the
beauty of the house that she had forgotten how much
she disapproved of the Marquis and his shocking plan
of marrying Christine so that he should continue his
liaison with Lady Lydford.

Now as she remembered that Barbara Castle-
maine had ben a mistress of Charles II and Lady
Lydford was the Marquis's, she felt he was insulting
Christine, and it made her angry.

There was a distinct pause before she said:

"I think ... My Lord, it would not be ... proper
for me to make ... personal remarks about my ...
relatives to a ... stranger."

For a moment the Marquis felt he could not have
heard her aright. Then, if all the golden ornaments on
the table had thrown themselves at him, he could not
have been more astonished.

That this young girl should tell him what was
proper and improper was surprising enough in itself,
but what made it worse was that he knew she was
right.

Of course it was a question he should not have
asked her, but it had never struck him for one moment
that Lord Lydford's daughter might be aware of his
feelings for her Stepmother and of hers for him.

Now he supposed that even though she was still
in the School-Room she must either have heard the
gossip circulating in the Social World or perhaps the
servants had talked in front of her.

Because the Marquis had spent many years at
Court, coping with awkward moments which might, if
not smoothed over quickly, lead to an international
incident, there was hardly a pause before he replied:

"Of course you are quite right, because although
I have known your father and Stepmother for a long
time, you and I have only just met."

Mina was not looking at him, but nevertheless he
smiled beguilingly as he went on:

"As you are now staying here as my guest, that is something which will soon be remedied, and I hope in any conversation we may have together in the future we will be able to talk to each other frankly and openly on any subject which is of interest to us both."

He thought as he spoke that he sounded somewhat priggish, but it was a definite effort to placate what he sensed was the hostile way in which Mina was regarding him.

'How could I have imagined,' he wondered to himself, 'that she would know about Nadine Lydford and me?'

Then he thought he had been extremely stupid in expecting her not to have sensed that there was someone besides her father in her Stepmother's life.

Also, he knew only too well how indiscreet women could be when they were in love.

They talked to their lady's-maids, their hairdressers, their intimate friends, and perhaps in this case even to their husband's daughter.

No-one knew better than he did how passionate and possessive Nadine's feelings were towards him and why she was trying to marry him to her Stepdaughter.

To have contrived so skilfully to get her to Vent Royal without his being able to refuse to take her was, to anyone perceptive, a revelation in itself.

'I must be careful how I handle this,' the Marquis thought, and continued:

"You will find here in my house a great quantity of paintings and furniture relating to the reign of Charles II. He was a Monarch whom I have always admired, and I shall be interested to hear what you think of the very fine portrait of him on the stairs."

"I have already noticed it," Mina replied, "and I like to remember that he was the first person to introduce ducks to London in St. James's Park."

"How are you aware of that?" the Marquis asked in surprise.

"He also provided the Park with a pair of pelicans."

"From Astrakhan, a present from the Russian Ambassador," the Marquis murmured.

He noticed that now that Mina was talking about birds, the hostility had left her eyes and once again she was speaking with a little lilt in her voice which he found very musical.

"Of course they are another type of bird, but why are you so interested in the ducks?" he enquired.

She was just about to say that as she lived in the fen country of Lincolnshire, the ducks which her father studied were very much a part of her daily life.

Just in time she remembered that she was supposed to be Christine, but after all there was no reason, as the Marquis had never met her, for Christine not to be interested in birds.

"I love all birds," she said in answer to his question. "But in particular, I think there is nothing more beautiful than seeing the ducks flighting in at dawn or at dusk."

"I agree with you," he said, "but I cannot believe you often get up so early to watch them."

"But I do, at the right time of year," Mina replied. "And do you know what I saw once?"

Because she felt the Marquis was interested, she could not prevent herself from telling him something which had happened during the last holiday she had spent at home before her father went abroad.

"What did you see?" he asked.

"Near where I was ... liv ... staying there was a pool in which there was a large pike. He was waiting to gobble up a batch of newly hatched ducklings, but I saw the mother carry them safely on her back until they reached the security of the shallows."

Mina spoke with an excited sincerity that made it obvious that she was telling the truth, but the Marquis stared at her incredulously.

"Have you really seen that yourself?" he asked. "I have heard that it happened, but I have always believed it was an old wives' tale."

"No, I actually saw it."

"Then you were very fortunate. It is something I would like to see myself."

Mina did not reply, as she was helping herself to another dish of what she was aware was particularly delicious and unusual food.

The Marquis asked:

"What other birds interest you?"

"If I say I want to study all of them, you will think I am setting myself a task which would take me years to achieve."

"That is certainly true," he answered. "Since I want to talk to you about your education, I should like to know your favourite subjects, apart from birds."

"If you are asking me what I would like to study, I would say Literature, which I am sure can be supplied by your Library, and the history of foreign countries of which I do not know nearly enough, especially Greece."

The Marquis raised his eye-brows.

"You consider those essential to your education?"

Mina nodded.

"I could compile a list of any other subjects if I could have teachers to help me."

She spoke a little wistfully, knowing that she would not be staying long enough to learn very much.

If she were really only sixteen it would have been exciting to think she had another year in which to study all the subjects that were available at Mrs. Fontwell's only to the pupils who could pay for them.

Because she was extremely intelligent, combined with the fact that she had spent so much time with her father, Mina had easily reached first place in the top form at the Seminary.

But she had found it disappointing that Mrs. Fontwell was far more concerned with teaching her pupils subjects which she considered to be social assets than those which taxed their brains.

French came into the former category, but not Greek. Latin was dismissed as quite unimportant, and a mere smattering of information about the Rulers of countries in Europe and their geographical locations was all that a Society débutante was likely to find useful.

Mina had wanted to learn so much more, and she thought now that if she could stay at Vent Royal long enough, she might find answers to hundreds of the questions that had received no reply when she had asked them at School.

"Perhaps you should give me a list of your requirements," the Marquis was saying, "then we can see what we can do about them. I suppose apart from book-learning you would like to have dancing-lessons."

"That is one thing we were taught well at School," Mina replied, "but I would love to fence, to ride, to practise archery, and to play tennis."

Again the Marquis looked surprised.

He had never considered fencing as a woman's sport, and he thought Mina looked too small and too fragile for what he felt was specifically a masculine skill.

Then he thought that with her grace of movement she might show the dexterity that made him one of the champion fencers of London.

"If we cannot find you a teacher here in the country," he said, "I suppose I shall have to teach you myself."

Mina's eyes lit up.

"Will you do that?" she asked. "I have often watched other people fencing, and I have learnt the right stance and essential movements. It is just that I have not been able to put them into practice."

Mina had longed to join the fencing classes,

which were another heavy expense to be added to
Mrs. Fontwell's bill.

She had watched every lesson that Christine had
received and had learnt every movement by heart.
She now thought it would be extremely exciting if the
Marquis taught her to fence with him.

"Fencing and tennis are not difficult," he said. "I
have a Court here and it is modelled exactly on the
one which was erected for Henry VIII, for whom, as I
expect you know, the game was invented."

"Yes indeed," Mina replied, "and again, I have
watched it very often but have not been able to
play."

This was certainly not a woman's game and Mrs.
Fontwell disapproved of it. But one or two of the
older girls had fathers who enjoyed Royal Tennis, as
it was called, and who were prepared for them to play
in the holidays.

When they were taken to the nearest Court,
which was at Windsor, Mina had gone with them as a
special privilege because Christine had insisted.

"I should have thought you were too small for
that game," the Marquis said.

"But I would like to try," Mina replied positively,
"and I am much stronger than I appear."

The Marquis smiled.

"You are certainly full of surprises, and it is quite
unnecessary for me to ask if you wish to ride my
horses, and, I presume, the most spirited."

"Now you are thought-reading," Mina answered,
and he laughed.

"I can see you will certainly have a lot to occupy
your days and will not be bored, as you might otherwise have been in the country."

"I would never be bored in the country."

There was silence for a moment. Then the Marquis said:

"I think I know the answer to that statement. You
are not bored or lonely because you have the birds
and the animals as companions."

73

He saw the answer in Mina's eyes and said:

"It is insulting to look so surprised. I am not as insensitive as you seem to think."

It was strange, he thought, that he felt he had to justify himself to this young girl who was not in the least what he had expected, and whose conversation was, to say the least of it, unusual.

All other women with whom he dined alone had always tried to entice him physically, to talk about themselves and their relationship with him.

Every subject he discussed with Mina was impersonal and yet to the Marquis extremely interesting.

Only as the servants left the room did he say:

"I can see that tomorrow you will be torn between deciding whether to go first to the stables or to the dove-cots where you can see my grandmother's doves."

"I particularly want to see them!" Mina said with a rapt little note in her voice.

"Why?" the Marquis asked, knowing the answer would be unexpected.

"They were the bird of Aphrodite," she replied, "and the Greeks appreciated their tenderness and their beauty."

"Aphrodite was of course the Goddess of Love."

As he spoke, he watched to see if Mina stiffened, as she had done before when he had inadvertently brought her Stepmother's name into the conversation.

But she seemed to be following her own thoughts as she said:

"The dove belonged to Aphrodite, the eagle to Zeus, and the peacock to Hera, spreading its tail of stars to the Queen of Heaven."

She smiled at the Marquis as she finished:

"And the duck to Poseidon, the Sea God."

"You are reminding me of things I thought I had forgotten long ago," the Marquis said. "But I think I am right in saying that for Apollo it was the swan."

"That is right," Mina approved, as if he had been

74

rather clever, "and he also had the hawk and the raven to carry his messages."

"Now I am beginning to understand why you think that we all resemble birds," the Marquis said. "And if you are a wren, which is a very modest little bird, which one would you attribute to me?"

Without considering, without thinking of what she should say, Mina replied:

"But of course, how could you be represented by anything but the eagle, King of the birds, and also a bird-of-prey?"

Even as she said the last words she wondered apprehensively if once again she had been rude.

She looked at the Marquis to see if he was offended.

"I understand your reasoning exactly, Mina," he said with a dry note in his voice, "but I think in making me a bird-of-prey you have forgotten something."

"What is that?"

"Far back in my mind I seem to remember reading or being told that peasants in Northern Europe swear that the eagle carried the golden crested wren, the smallest of the family to which you think you belong, safely tucked away among the feathers on his back on flights over hundreds of miles of swamp and sea towards the Northern wastelands."

Mina gave a little cry and clasped her hands together.

"I remember hearing that too," she said. "There is no reason why it should not be possible, and it is a lovely idea!"

She was obviously thrilled by it, and the Marquis realised that she was considering it quite impersonally.

She did not for a moment think, as any other woman would have done, that metaphorically he might carry her!

● ● ●

The Marquis was not surprised the following morning when he reached the stables to find Mina already there.

He had in fact told her before they retired to bed that if she wanted to ride, she had only to order a horse and his Head Groom would know which one was most suitable for her.

"Do you think he would let me choose for myself?" Mina asked.

"I think he might be rather apprehensive."

"I hope he will soon learn to trust me," Mina said simply.

They had reached the Hall while they had been talking. She curtseyed to the Marquis and added:

"Thank you, My Lord. It has been a very, very interesting evening."

She had gone upstairs, and as he watched her go the Marquis had been aware that once again she was doing the unexpected by not looking back.

Any other woman would have leant flirtatiously over the bannisters at the top of the staircase to say a last good-night.

But Mina had gone straight on towards her bedroom, and the Marquis had the extraordinary idea that she had already forgotten his existence.

As he walked to the Library he thought it had been an evening of so many surprises that he had ceased to count them.

First of all, he was aware that Mina's appearance of being little more than a child certainly belied her.

She was not only much more intelligent than he had expected but a great deal more knowledgeable.

As dinner had progressed and they had spoken again of Charles II, he was surprised to find that she had a knowledge of the King's life which could only have come from a great deal of reading on the subject.

His foreign policies, his scientific interests, his

walking, hunting, and racing were all things that Mina could discuss with the Marquis, besides his opinions on absolutism, astrology, and the Dutch.

"How can you know so much about him?" the Marquis finally asked when they had talked of the claustrophobia from which the King had suffered.

"I have always found Charles II the most fascinating of the English Kings," Mina said simply, "and while the other girls were mainly interested in Nell Gwynn and Louise de Keroualle, I always thought he was so much more than a mere Rake."

As she spoke she remembered that she had thought the Marquis was a Rake, and he saw the colour rise in her cheeks and guessed the reason for it.

He wanted to challenge her by asking her who had told her he was one, then he decided it was too soon.

She had snubbed him once for being too personal, and he was not going to lay himself open again to such a reproach.

To his surprise, he had found himself lying awake and thinking over the subjects they had discussed, but now as he saw her in the stables, looking so ridiculously young, he told himself that he must have imagined their conversations.

They could only have taken place not with a woman but with a man.

"Good-mornin', M'Lord," the old groom said as the Marquis approached; and Mina, who had been busy patting one of the horses, turned her head.

"Good-morning, Abbey," the Duke said. "Good-morning, Mina! Have you chosen the horse you wish to ride?"

Mina glanced at the groom and he said:

"It's loik this, M'Lord. The young Lady wants to ride Firefly, but Oi don't consider 'im a suitable mount, nor a safe one."

"I certainly had trouble with him myself the last

77

time I rode him," the Marquis agreed, "so I think, Mina, you must choose again."

"I seem to remember, My Lord, you promised me that I could ride whichever horse I fancied," Mina reminded him, "and I would be prepared to bet you, if I had any money, that Firefly will behave with me!"

She realised as she finished speaking that once again she had made a slip.

She hoped that the Marquis would not notice or that he would simply think she had meant that she had no money with her.

However, because she felt nervous at being so foolish as to forget that she was supposed to be Christine, she turned away from the stall where she had been patting the horse which Abbey wished her to ride, and walked to the end stall where Firefly was snorting and neighing because he was not receiving sufficient attention.

The Marquis thought afterwards that what happened was only to be expected, in the light of his learning the night before how much birds and animals meant to Mina.

She walked boldly into Firefly's stall while Abbey muttered warnings beneath his breath.

She talked to the great horse, patted him, and apparently coaxed him into a good humour before he allowed himself to be saddled.

Outside in the stable-yard, as the Marquis lifted her onto the saddle, he was worried in case she was assuming an unjustified confidence and the horse which had almost pulled his arms out of their sockets would bolt with her.

Mina had smiled at him reassuringly as if he were behaving like an over-anxious Nanny and trotted off so that the Marquis had to mount his own horse quickly to catch up with her.

Afterwards he could hardly believe that their ride, as far as the horses were concerned, had been so smooth and uneventful.

What Mina of course had not told him was that

because her father had been so hard-up, he had bought unbroken horses and she had helped him break them in.

She had learnt from him the special magic he had in taming untrained animals so that from the moment he handled them they trusted him and the battle was over before it began.

That Mina rode well went without saying, and the Marquis appreciated her straight little back, the way she held her reins, and the manner in which she continually talked to her horse.

It surprised him all the more because he could not remember ever hearing that Lord Lydford was a particularly outstanding horseman, and he knew that Nadine was what was called a "Park trotter" and rode as seldom as possible.

As they rode home after galloping the freshness out of their mounts and bringing a glow to Mina's cheeks, the Marquis knew that this was one lesson in which he might learn more than he could teach.

"I suspect you of being a white witch," he said as the house came into sight, "who has cast a magic spell over Firefly. He has been difficult ever since I bought him."

"He is a magnificent horse!" Mina replied. "It is because they are frightened of him that he behaves badly."

"That may be true," the Marquis admitted, "but he has tried to kick his stall down and injured a groom who was laid up for a fortnight."

"I will teach him how to behave."

"How?"

"I do not think I can exactly put it into words," Mina answered after a moment, "but ..."

She was just going ot say: "Papa could control any animal he wished to," when once again she remembered who she was supposed to be.

"But—what?" the Marquis questioned.

"As you pointed out to me last night," Mina replied, "I am here to learn."

79

"Now you are being infuriatingly evasive. Take care, or your teacher may have to punish you!"

"And how would you do that?" Mina enquired.

"I always think the punishment should fit the crime," the Marquis replied, "and I have the feeling the one you would dislike most would be if I stopped you from riding, or shut you up in your bedroom where you could not be with the birds."

"If you did that, I should fly away."

"As an eagle I would bring you back."

She laughed.

"But first you would have to find me. Have you forgotten that the wren is a small, insignificant creature? You would sweep imperiously overhead without seeing me tucked away in my nest, hidden at the bottom of a bush or a straggling hedgerow."

"You underestimate me," the Marquis said, "but I hope it is something we shall not have to put to the test."

They were both speaking lightly, almost jokingly, but it struck Mina that the day might come when "many a word spoken in jest" would prove true.

If she ran away from Vent Royal, one thing was quite certain—the Marquis would not follow her, nor, she thought, would he even be interested to know where she had gone.

But for the moment all that mattered was that she could ride his horses and explore a most fascinating and beautiful place that seemed like Paradise, the Garden of Eden itself.

They ate breakfast as soon as they returned to the house. Then Mina went upstairs to change from her riding-habit and the Marquis went to the Library.

His secretary was waiting for him with a pile of letters to sign and a list of people on the Estate who wished to see him.

It was several hours later before he had finished and Mr. Caruthers said there was no further business demanding his attention.

It was then that he thought of Mina, and, going into the Hall, he asked the Butler where she was.

"Miss Lydford was with Her Ladyship for some-time, M'Lord," the Butler replied, "and when Her Ladyship was getting up, she came downstairs and went into the garden."

"That was where I expected her to be," the Marquis said, and walked to where there was a garden-door to let him out on the south side of the house.

He expected to find Mina with his grandmother's doves, but she was not there, and he walked on through the yew-hedges with their strange, ancient examples of topiary towards the walled gardens that were a feature of the grounds.

There was the herb-garden, the gold-fish garden, and near the woods a water-lily pool with its cascade tumbling down over rocks that were partly artificial and partly belonged to the natural formation of the rising ground.

The Marquis entered the garden through bushes of syringa which were in full flower and whose scent filled the air.

Then as he saw Mina on the edge of the pool he stood still.

She was sitting on a moss-covered rock and he saw that perched on her raised hands were several small birds.

The Marquis recognised a chaffinch and a house-martin, then he saw that on her knee there was a robin.

Although he could hear no sound, he felt that she was talking to them. They were quite unafraid and put their heads to one side as if they listened to her.

In her gown of pale green that seemed to blend with the shrubs and the grass, she made a picture which the Marquis felt was more beautiful than anything he had seen on canvass.

Then one of his dogs which had accompanied

him but had trailed behind came rushing up. The noise he made disturbed the birds and they flew away. Mina turned to see who was there.

"How can you do that?" the Marquis asked. "Why did those birds come to you when you were not even feeding them?"

"It is something I have always been able to do," she replied, "ever since I was small."

"And why can I not do the same thing?"

"I think perhaps you could, but you have to call them."

"Call them? You mean whistle for them?"

She shook her head.

"Then how?" he insisted.

He thought she was not going to tell him, finding it difficult to explain, but after a moment she said:

"I send my . . . thoughts towards . . . them."

"You mean that draws them?"

"I think perhaps it is like a note of music which we both hear, and they know that it means I want to be friendly and so they come to me."

Then she made a helpless little gesture with her hands.

"I am explaining it badly, but it is thought that applies to whatever we do—people, animals, birds."

She gave a little laugh as she added:

"I am not so sure with fish. The water makes it difficult to reach them."

"I find it very fascinating that you should have this gift," he said, "if that is what it is."

"I think perhaps the right word is 'magic'."

"Very well then, magic," he said. "Do you realise that in a less civilised age you might have been burnt as a witch?"

"I once tried to attract a cat," Mina said, "but dogs are different."

The Marquis had been aware that while he was talking, his spaniel was nestling against Mina, inviting her to pat her.

She touched his head gently with her fingers and it seemed to evoke an ecstatic emotion from him.

The Marquis sat down on a rock near to where Mina was sitting.

"I thought yesterday that a very young and doubtless very ignorant young woman would be arriving here," he said. "Now I feel that I am the one who is ignorant."

"You are fishing for compliments," Mina replied. "You know as well as I do that you are extremely knowledgeable on subjects about which I know nothing and for which I have unfortunately never had a teacher."

It shot through the Marquis's mind that she would be not only very easy to teach but very alluring.

Then he told himself that it was far too soon to make a decision of that sort, and he was in fact just exploring his way into what was to him a new world.

He looked up at the tree above them, almost as if he expected to see a number of birds waiting to fly down to Mina if he were not there.

She knew what he was doing and smiled.

"You frightened them away and it will take sometime for them to return, even if I were alone," she explained.

"But you can call all the birds in the same way?"

"Only the ones I want. Those I do not want know they are not welcome and do not answer my secret call."

She considered for a moment before she said:

"I suppose, although I try to understand them, that starlings and sparrows are not my favourites."

"Why not?" the Marquis asked.

"Because they are born robbers and burglars, quarrelsome, noisy, and vulgar."

The Marquis laughed.

"They are certainly in your bad books! And what others?"

"The cuckoo, of course," Mina replied. "His life is one long history of burglary, robbery, murder, and plain blackguardism."

"I must agree with you there," the Marquis replied, "but I have never heard anyone put the case quite so vehemently against him."

"He kills all the baby birds in the nest where he has intruded. Then his foster-parents become his slaves, and, until he is big enough to fly, they have the unending drudgery of having to find food for that great gaping bully who has murdered their young!"

The Marquis laughed again.

"You are making your birds seem more real to me than some human beings."

"That is what they are to me," Mina said. "But I suppose because I have been so much alone they have taken the place of people."

She saw the surprise in the Marquis's eyes and realised that once again she was speaking as herself.

Because she was embarrassed, she got off the rock on which she had been sitting.

"I think perhaps I should go back to the house," she said. "I expect it is nearly luncheon-time."

"You are right," the Marquis agreed. "And you must tell me what you would like to do after we have eaten—unless of course you want to rest?"

"How could I waste time doing anything so foolish when there is so much to explore?" Mina replied.

"Then I will take you driving," he said. "There is a great deal to see besides the garden."

He was waiting for Mina to say how much this would please her, and when she did not speak, he realised that she was looking ahead of them to where she could see the dove-cots.

The Marchioness's white doves seen against the mellow walls of Vent Royal looked like something out of a fairy-story, and as Mina walked towards them several of them flew up into the air and fluttered overhead as if they had come to greet her.

Instinctively the Marquis stood still and Mina

moved on a few paces, then flung up her arms towards them, tipping her head back as if she called them.

They fluttered down, one on each of her hands, two others on her shoulders, while others seemed content to cluster round her feet.

It was so lovely, so spontaneous and unexpected, and the Marquis knew he had never thought to see anything like it in his own garden.

And yet there was a rightness about it, just as if in some strange way it had happened many times before and was part of the flowers, the garden, the sky overhead, and Vent Royal itself.

It was as if he had stepped back in time and he was seeing a picture that had existed somewhere all down the centuries.

Perhaps it was at the very beginning of Creation, when the Goddess Aphrodite, to whom the doves had been dedicated, had come down from Olympus to make them hers.

Chapter Five

Mina came into the Marchioness's Sitting-Room holding something in her hand and reached the centre of the room before she realised that the Marchioness was not alone. As the Marquis rose to his feet, she said hastily:

"I am so sorry. I did not mean to interrupt, but I wanted your grandmother to see this dove."

As she moved forward, the Marchioness exclaimed:

"Oh, you have found the one that was lost!"

"The gardeners had done that, Ma'am," Mina answered, "but he has broken his leg."

"How terrible!" the Marchioness cried. "Can nothing be done for him?"

"I have put a splint on it," Mina said, "and I thought you would like to see it. I am sure it will heal if we keep him shut up for about a week."

The pigeon was lying unafraid, cradled in Mina's arms, as she carried him close to the Marchioness so she could see that his leg had a tiny splint on it and was now straight.

"It is beautifully done!" the Marchioness approved. "How clever of you, Mina, to know what to do!"

"I have had a lot of practice with broken legs and broken wings," Mina explained.

As she spoke, she was thinking of the ducks, plovers, and swallows that her father had treated at home.

Many of those which flew hundreds of miles from

far-off lands arrived exhausted and injured themselves on landing.

Then, as if she felt she had been unwise to admit to such knowledge, she said quickly:

"I will take the dove back. He is feeling much better now that he has been fed and has a comfortable place to lie. But he must not try to walk about or fly until his leg is stronger."

"No, of course not," the Marchioness said with a smile.

She did not attempt to touch the pigeon, knowing that while doves were very tame with Mina, they were nervous with anybody else.

Mina looked at the Marquis.

"I am sorry to interrupt."

"I will see you later," the Marquis answered, and she smiled at him before she left the room.

"That child has a fantastic way with birds," the Marchioness said.

"She has indeed," the Marquis agreed.

"And with everyone else, for that matter," the Marchioness went on. "Agnes keeps telling me how the servants adore her, and I hear old Abbey talks of nothing but the way she manages to control Firefly."

"It is true," the Marquis said. "She certainly has an exceptional power over horses as well as birds."

In the garden, as Mina put the injured dove into a small cage which the gardeners had constructed for it, she thought of how her father would have been pleased by the skill with which she had treated its leg.

There were so many things at Vent Royal that would have delighted her father.

Every day she wished not once but a hundred times that she could show him the birds and other animals with which she spent her time when she was not with the Marquis.

Then she thought she had never been as happy as she had been this past week, and knew with a little pang that it would be hard to leave Vent Royal.

She forced herself not to think about it, knowing

that the moment Christine wrote to her that she was married, she must go and if possible without seeing the Marquis before she left.

"He will be angry ... very angry that I have ... deceived him," she told herself apprehensively.

Then she tried not to think about it, knowing that to do so would spoil the excitement of the days that never seemed long enough because there was so much to do, to see, and to learn.

One thing that was more exciting than anything else was that she was trying to tame a roe deer.

Her father had told her that a roe deer was the most intelligent of all the deers, having twice the brains, twice the wits, and twice the sense and faculties of the red deer.

"The red deer are polygamous," he had said to Mina, "but the roe has only one wife and sticks to her."

"And do you think that makes him more clever than the others?" Mina asked.

"All the records show," he replied, "that monogamous animals have about double the intelligence of those which are promiscuous lovers, and that is, I am sure, why the roe deer survives."

He had gone on to say that no animal was better camouflaged by nature.

"The roe deer," he explained, "can stand facing you against a bank of bracken in broad daylight and you will not see him, and at night you will not hear him."

Mina had been very interested at the time, but now she wondered if what her father had said about the deer applied also to human beings.

Though she had certainly been shocked by the stories of the Marquis's love-life, she could not say he was unintelligent.

In fact, she found him brilliantly clever, with a logical answer to every question she asked him, and sometimes too he spoke to her in a way that her father might have done.

When he talked about Greece he seemed to understand how the classical Greeks had revolutionised the thinking of mankind all those centuries ago, and that their influence still survives today.

Every time she and the Marquis talked together, she felt as if her thoughts reached out to him and that while he stimulated her mind, sometimes she did the same to him.

The roe deer—and the Marquis admitted there were very few of them left in the Park—were very elusive, although one of the younger ones was beginning to trust Mina and drew nearer and nearer to her each day.

When the Marquis left his grandmother, he went downstairs and found his way to the Library.

He had arranged with Mina earlier that after riding they would study for at least an hour the history of Persia. She had already found some books on the shelves and there was a pile of them on the Marquis's desk.

Although he had talked about providing her with teachers, he said he had so far not been able to find one whom he considered capable of teaching the subjects Mina wanted to study.

Instead he had concentrated on giving her fencing-lessons, which she adored, and discussing with her, as she had wished, the countries of the world that had a centuries-old history which had affected the progress of civilisation.

Because it was now ten years since he had come down from Oxford, the Marquis was afraid that he might prove lamentably ignorant.

But fortunately, being a great reader, he had not been at an obvious disadvantage when confronted by a girl who was insatiable for knowledge.

He found himself extremely intrigued by Mina and constantly wondered what she would ask him next.

It was a new experience to be treated as if he were a human encyclopaedia which she was confident would provide the right answer to every question.

89

What was an even more unusual experience was that when they were working together, and at other times too, Mina never treated him as if he was an attractive man.

He knew there was something about him which frightened her at times. Moreover, when there was a reference in any way to her Stepmother, she stiffened, and there was a look of shocked disgust in her eyes which definitely perturbed him.

Otherwise, she was as unselfconscious and natural with him as if he were old enough to be her father, as she was also at ease with his grandmother, for whom she had an easy friendliness which the Marquis envied.

He had never expected, after his long experience with women, that he would find one who would be to him an enigma, though on the surface she was nothing but a very young if very attractive girl.

Every day that they were together he found himself discovering new aspects of her personality that he had not noticed before.

Meanwhile, it surprised his grandmother that he had not returned to the amusements of London but seemed content to be at Vent Royal with Mina.

When he came into the Library now, he appreciated that the sunshine coming through one of the long windows made her fair hair glow like a halo, and there was also a light in her eyes that he had grown to look for when she saw him.

"I have found some more books," she cried, "and an absolutely fascinating one with pictures of mosaics which I would give anything in the world to see!"

"You will have to consider taking a voyage to the East," the Marquis said.

"I would love that," Mina answered.

Then she knew it was something she could never afford, and also that it was the East that had taken her father from her. At the thought, a shadow passed over her face, which the Marquis noticed, and he hoped she would explain to him the reason for it.

He knew instinctively that it was part of the secret Mina would not share with him, and while he waited hopefully, he feared that she would remain as elusive as the roe deer and would offer him no explanation.

He watched her as she picked up one of the books from the desk.

"Do come and look at what I have found!" she cried, and the Marquis knew that the moment in which she might have confided in him had passed.

He was about to sit down at his desk when the door of the Library opened and the Butler said in a rather flustered voice:

"Lady Bartlett, M'Lord!"

The way Eloise Bartlett swept into the room told the Marquis that she had forced her way into the house despite being told by the servants, on his instructions, that he was "not at home."

She was looking exceedingly beautiful in a gown of strawberry-pink silk, rucked, tucked, and ornamented with lace, which revealed her exquisite figure.

Her hat was trimmed with flowers and small ostrich-feathers, and every time she moved she glittered with the diamonds she wore in her ears and on her bodice and wrists.

She swept up to the Marquis, seeming taller than she usually did because she was angry, and it showed itself in the darkness of her eyes and in the determination of her raised chin.

"I have called to see you, Tian," she said, "because I am tired of sending you notes that are not answered, and I wish to know why you are ignoring me."

She did not wait for the Marquis to reply, but turned her head to look at Mina, who was staring at her wide-eyed, holding a book in her hand.

"So it is true that Nadine Lydford has foisted her Stepchild onto you!" she said sharply. "I had heard a rumour that was so, but I could not believe it. For what reason have you started a Kindergarten at Vent Royal?"

91

Her tone of voice conveyed a very unpleasant innuendo.

The Marquis, apparently quite unmoved by her tirade and her unexpected appearance, said quietly:

"Good-morning, Eloise! It is a surprise to see you, but it is kind of you to call."

"I am not being kind!" Lady Bartlett snapped. "I want an explanation as to why you have not been in touch with me, and I intend to have one!"

"Before we concern ourselves with anything of a personal nature," the Marquis said, still speaking in a quiet, calm voice, "may I present Mina, who, as you have heard quite correctly, is Lord Lydford's daughter."

"And Nadine Lydford's Stepdaughter!"

"As you say. It is no secret."

"You have kept it a secret from me that she was here," Lady Bartlett retorted, "and I believed, even if you did not say so in so many words, that you had finished with Nadine Lydford when she left for India."

The innuendo was so obvious that for the first time since her appearance the Marquis frowned and there was an expression of anger in his eyes.

He turned to Mina.

"I think," he said, "we will have to postpone our studies until a later hour."

His words broke the spell which had left Mina standing motionless, feeling almost as if she were holding her breath.

Without looking at either the Marquis or Lady Bartlett, she put the books she was holding down on the desk and moved quickly towards the door.

As she reached it and put out her hand to open it, Lady Bartlett said scornfully:

"I cannot understand, Tian, how you can waste your time with an unfledged chit when we might be . . ."

Mina did not wait to hear any more.

She went from the Library, shut the door behind

her, then ran as quickly as she could out through an
open door which led onto the lawn, and still running
crossed the bridge over the lake to disappear amongst
the trees in the Park.

In the Library there was silence as Lady Bartlett
waited for an answer to her question.

Then slowly and deliberately the Marquis said in
an icy voice that was as cutting as a whip:

"I find it extremely surprising, Eloise, that as my
neighbour and your husband's wife you should come
here, making a scene which to say the least of it is
extremely indiscreet!"

Lady Bartlett gave an audible little gasp.

"Can you really be speaking to me in such a
manner?" she enquired.

"I am thinking both of your reputation and of my
own," the Marquis said. "I suggest, Eloise, that you
should understand that I have your interests at heart
when I remind you, as you appear to have forgotten,
that in the country gossip travels on the wind."

As if she suddenly realised she had made a mistake in attacking the Marquis, Eloise Bartlett changed
her tactics and moved nearer to him to say:

"Forgive me, Tian. I know I was wrong to speak
to you as I did, but I have been so unhappy, so
distraught, because I have not heard from you."

Her voice softened and her face was so beautiful
as she looked up at the Marquis with appealing,
contrite eyes that it seemed extraordinary that he
could regard her without a flicker of interest in his
own eyes.

"I have waited and waited," Eloise Bartlett went
on, "praying that I should hear from you, and even
sitting in the evenings in our secret place, hoping you
would come to me."

She contrived a little sob on the last words, but
the Marquis was unmoved.

"There are very good reasons for my not doing
so," he said coldly, "and I think, Eloise, that we are
both too sophisticated and too experienced to imagine

that reproaches or recriminations will achieve anything."

There was a long silence. Then Lady Bartlett asked:

"Are you telling me that I am no longer—attractive?"

She said the word almost as if it was utterly impossible for it to be true, and, having said it, she waited for the Marquis to deny the suggestion.

Instead he said:

"You are very beautiful, Eloise, as you are well aware, and I shall always think with great gratitude of the happiness you have given me."

"You mean—it is over?" Eloise Bartlett gasped. "I do not believe it!"

She held out her arms to him as she spoke, but the Marquis, without appearing to have done so, had somehow retreated behind his desk.

"May I offer you some refreshment before you return home?" he enquired.

Lady Bartlett's eyes searched his face as if he were a stranger whom she had never seen before. Then she said in a strangled tone:

"You are sending me—away, and still I cannot—believe it! What has happened? Who has made trouble? How can you possibly treat me like—this, after all we have—meant to each other?"

"It would be the greatest mistake," the Marquis said after a pause, "to spoil memories which we should both cherish."

As if with an effort, Lady Bartlett prevented herself from speaking the words of fury that came into her mind.

For a moment she contemplated screaming at the Marquis, then she knew that he would only be contemptuous of what he would consider a vulgar lack of self-control.

Instead, she drew a small handkerchief from her waist-band and put it to her eyes.

"You have—hurt me, Tian," she said in a broken

voice. "I—loved you as I have never—loved another man in my whole—life—and I cannot imagine that you—no longer care for me."

As she spoke she sat down on the sofa as if her legs would no longer support her.

It would have been more moving if she had not arranged herself so carefully in her effort to appear unhappy and brokenhearted.

The Marquis did not move from behind his desk. He only watched her as she applied a handkerchief to her eyes, but there was not a smudge on the thin layer of powder which she used very artistically on her fair skin.

For a moment nobody spoke, then the Marquis said:

"Let me offer you a glass of champagne before you leave. It will revive you, Eloise, after this harrowing scene, and I think it would be a mistake for the servants to see that you are crying."

Lady Bartlett took the handkerchief away from her eyes.

"You are behaving extremely badly, Tian, as you well know," she said angrily. "But I shall find out why you have changed towards me, and when I know who it is, I promise you I shall scratch her eyes out!"

The Marquis gave a little laugh.

"Bravo, Eloise!" he said. "I like you when you are natural! You are far more effective as Brunhilda charging into battle than as weeping Phoebe bemoaning those she has lost!"

As he spoke, he could not help thinking that Eloise Bartlett would have not the slightest idea who the characters were to whom he had referred, while Mina would appreciate how aptly they had been chosen.

Lady Bartlett put her handkerchief into her waist-band and rose to her feet.

"As you are mocking me and I am obviously not wanted, I will leave," she said. "But one day, Tian, I will get even with you, while I shall pray every night of my life that you will suffer as you have made me suffer, and of course a great many other women before me."

She lifted her head with a dignity that the Marquis attributed to good acting and walked towards the door.

She walked slowly enough for him to reach it before she did, and as he opened it she sailed out of the Library with a flutter of feathers and a rustle of her silk gown.

He escorted her to the front door in silence, but as she walked down the steps to her carriage, the Marquis said in a voice loud enough to be heard by his Butler, the footmen, and the Bartlett coachman:

"Please carry my respects to His Lordship and thank him most sincerely for the information you have brought me. Assure him that it was exactly what I was waiting for, and I am extremely grateful."

Lady Bartlett made no effort to support the Marquis's explanation for her presence.

Instead, she allowed him to help her into the carriage, and while her fingers lingered on his for a moment longer than was necessary, she was well aware that the gesture evoked no response in him.

Then as he stepped back, the footman closed the door and the horses started off.

The Marquis raised his hand in farewell, but Lady Bartlett merely stared ahead of her with a stony expression on her face.

As he walked back to the house, the Marquis's grey eyes were stormy.

If there was one thing he really disliked, it was a scene, and he had imagined that Eloise Bartlett had more pride than to lower herself to behave in such a manner.

If she was angry, resentful, and hurt all at the same time, it was nothing new.

In the past the Marquis had endured quite a number of similar scenes from the women he had discarded, but they had usually taken place in London, where there was no chance of their creating such a spate of gossip as there would be in the ountry.

He could only hope that what he had said about receiving information from Lord Bartlett would be repeated to their other servants when Eloise arrived home and would also be circulated at Vent Royal.

But that still left Mina!

He thought it could not have been more unfortunate, just when he had hoped she was beginning to forget the situation between her Stepmother and himself, that Eloise should have behaved in such an outrageous manner.

He felt inclined to curse her for her behaviour, but he had the honesty to admit that it was his own fault.

He should never have become intimate in the first place with the wife of so near a neighbour, his only excuse being that she was very beautiful and had done everything she could to entice him.

" 'The woman tempted me,' " the Marquis quoted to himself with a wry smile.

He knew that the most difficult part of making reparation for the past lay immediately ahead of him.

He had to find Mina, and he was certain she would not be in the house but would have gone out into the garden.

He went first to where the white doves were cooing and preening themselves on the roofs of their dove-cots, but there was no sign of her.

He was not surprised, because he thought that if, as he suspected, she had been shocked by the things that Eloise Bartlett had said, she would have gone farther afield.

He knew that the most likely place was where she was trying to tame the roe deer, and he walked over the bridge which spanned the lake and turned left.

Sheltered by shrubs and trees, there was a very quiet, rather isolated part of the Park where few people ever went except for himself, and now Mina.

He moved silently over the thick grass until, as he had expected, he saw her some distance away.

She was seated on the ground, her white skirts billowing round her, and about six feet from her was a roe deer.

It stood not much higher than his waist, and its head had only six points, but it had a grace and beauty that remained him of Mina herself.

Mina was looking at it, and he knew she was sending out her thoughts, using what she called her "magic" to draw the animal nearer and nearer to her.

She used a spell which was part of Creation itself and was perhaps known when the first man came on earth.

It had been forgotten later, when he turned away from the spiritual knowledge that was part of his inheritance to study matters more physical and mundane.

The Marquis stood watching, but the mere fact that he was there soon made the roe deer conscious of him.

It turned its head to sniff the air, and a moment later, swifter than thought, it was gone and had vanished among the trees as if it had been nothing but a fantasy.

The Marquis moved forward, and although Mina did not turn her head or move, he knew she was aware that he was approaching her.

When he reached her he sat down beside her, stretching himself out on the grass so that his elbow supported him and his head rested on his hand.

Her head was bent and her eyes were downcast as she looked at her fingers clasped together in her lap. She did not fidget or move as anyone else might have done.

The Marquis did not speak, he only looked at her,

and after a long silence, with only the whisper of the leaves in the trees overhead and the crickets chirping in the grass, he said:

"I am sorry, Mina!"

She did not answer but he knew what she was thinking, and after a moment he went on:

"I know you are shocked, but because you are well read, you must be aware that such things have happened since the beginning of time."

Again there was silence. Then at length, as if he compelled her to answer him, she said, the words almost inaudible:

"She is . . . married!"

The Marquis knew then that she was thinking not only of Lady Bartlett but also of her Stepmother.

"So was Queen Guinevere," he said quietly, "and Cleopatra and Helen of Troy. There is no need for me to add to the list. You can do that for yourself."

She raised her eye-lids for one brief second, and he realised that this aspect had not occurred to her before. Then she added:

"It is . . . wrong."

"Of course it is, morally speaking," he agreed, "but life is short, and human beings seek happiness wherever they can find it, just as your animals do."

He felt that she was not quite so tense, and he continued:

"I cannot believe you would turn away from a wounded pheasant which has half-a-dozen wives or from numerous other birds which are extremely promiscuous and, from your point of view, extremely immoral."

As if Mina could not help contributing to the conversation, because they had argued and talked on so many subjects, she said:

"Rooks . . . seldom have more than . . . one wife."

As if he thought he had broken through the invisible barrier with which she had surrounded herself, the Marquis gave a little laugh.

"That is true, and an old Keeper used to tell me when I was a boy that if a libertine, or perhaps you would call him a Rake, assaults the nesting wife of another bird, the whole colony comes down on him like a ton of bricks."

"They have a ... Court ... Martial."

"Exactly!" the Marquis agreed. "And I was told that first one rook, then another will caw against him. Finally, when the Court's verdict has been reached, the offender is mobbed, pecked, driven out, and sometimes harried to death!"

He knew that Mina was listening, and he said very softly:

"Is that what you want done to me?"

He waited, hoping she would respond and yet uncertain what her verdict where he was concerned would be.

Then suddenly, not far from where they were sitting, there was the sound of a gun-shot.

It seemed to explode almost ear-shatteringly in the silence, and both Mina and the Marquis jumped instinctively to their feet.

Without even speaking to each other, they both started to run in the direction from which the sound had come, and as they did so they saw a herd of spotted deer sprinting wildly across the grass as if in panic.

It was only a short distance for the Marquis and Mina to run before they saw what had occurred.

Through the tree-trunks they could see a man holding an old-fashioned, long-barrelled gun in his hands, and lying at his feet on the grass was an animal.

Simultaneously he saw them, and just as the deer had run away he moved too, running, jumping over fallen boughs, moving with a speed that showed he was both young and active.

By the time Mina and the Marquis had reached what was lying on the ground, the man was out of sight.

Then they saw that a spotted doe which was in calf was lying on the ground.

She had been shot in the heart, and her muscles were still twitching but her eye-lids with their long, child-like lashes were closing over her frightened eyes.

"A poacher!" the Marquis said furiously.

As he spoke, Mina knelt down for a moment beside the doe and touched its neck.

As if she knew it was hopeless and there was nothing she could do, she rose to her feet again.

"H-how could ... anybody do anything so ... cruel?" she cried.

Then instinctively, as if in need of comfort not only for herself but for the fallen animal, she turned towards the Marquis and hid her face against his shoulder.

He could feel her trembling against him and he put his arms round her.

As he did so, he knew that he was in love, deeply, overwhelmingly, whole-heartedly in love, as he had never been before in his whole life!

He wanted to protect Mina, to look after her, to keep her from all contact with anything that was cruel or ugly, unpleasant or wrong.

He could not explain to himself how the conviction that this was what he wanted swept over him like a tidal-wave. He only knew it was there, indescribably and positively.

At the same time, there was something ecstatic in the knowledge of what he felt, which aroused his mind and—although it was a very strange thing for him to think—his soul.

He wanted to say: "I love you, and I will never let anything, man, woman, or beast, hurt you again," but he knew that would upset her more than she was already.

He could only hold her very close to him, hoping that his arms were comforting, and knowing she was fighting against bursting into tears.

Again with an instinct he had never used before, he knew that she was thinking not of her own feelings but those of the doe.

After a moment he said quietly:

"She did not suffer. She was shot in the heart and it was almost instantaneous."

"She was ... so ... beautiful."

"Poachers are only concerned with what money they can get, not with what they kill," the Marquis said, "but I will see that the Game-keepers are on the look-out for that man and any more like him."

His voice deepened with anger as he went on:

"This is something which has not happened in the Park for a very long time, and I suspect the poacher, if he is a local man, expected me to be away from home at this time of the year."

He was talking to give Mina time to compose herself, but he still held her against him.

She was so slight and small, and he knew that while she was only a child, at the same time she was the woman he had always imagined he might one day find for himself.

"I have found you! I have found you!" he wanted to tell her. "And in my dreams you existed as you are now."

But he knew that not only was Mina far too young for him to say such things to her, but also he had already shocked her not once but twice.

She was shocked, perhaps disgusted, by his behaviour with her Stepmother, and she had been deeply shocked in realising that Eloise Bartlett was another Barbara Castlemaine in his life.

He found himself remembering how horrified Catherine de Braganza had been when, after her arrival in England, she first met the King's mistress.

When the notorious Barbara was first presented to her, Catherine's eyes filled with tears of rage, her nose began to bleed, and she collapsed on the floor in hysterics.

The King had shrugged his shoulders and sent

Lord Carrington to reason with her. She soon discovered that hysteria and threats were no way to behave where her husband was concerned.

As the Marquis held Mina closer, it flashed through his mind that in a similar situation her behaviour had been very different.

Although she was very young, she had a self-control and a dignity which he admired.

He knew that whatever he did, she would not rage at him, just as now at the slaughter of one of her beloved animals she was not screaming or even crying.

She was showing a fortitude which told him what he knew already—that she had a strong character that was very unusual in somebody so young and so unsophisticated.

Without her being aware of it, his lips touched her hair, and he told himself that he was the most fortunate man in the world to have found his ideal when he had thought it impossible for her even to exist.

Now he felt like Jason discovering the Golden Fleece or perhaps Sir Galahad sighting the Holy Grail.

He wanted to proclaim not only to Mina but to the whole world that she belonged to him.

Then, because he had learnt to control his feelings and he knew that she was as wary and untamed as the roe deer that had just vanished, he said quietly:

"Shall we go back and find the Game-keepers?"

Mina raised her head from his shoulder.

"Y-yes."

She turned round to look at the doe lying in the grass with her eyes now closed. She might have been peacefully asleep.

The Marquis took Mina's hand.

"Come,' he said. "She is already on some Elysian field where the grass is always green and where there are no mortals with the lust to destroy."

Mina's fingers tightened on his.

"People ... say that ... animals and birds do ... not go to ... Heaven."

"But we know they do," the Marquis replied. "Otherwise for you it would not be Heaven, would it?"

She smiled and it was like the sun coming through the clouds.

"No, of course not!" she answered. "And that is the answer I have ... always wanted to ... hear."

Chapter Six

As they sat at dinner in the Dining-Room, the Marquis thought that Mina looked unusually pale but very beautiful.

He had been thinking as he dressed what a shock it must have been for her to hear the doe being shot and to be there at the very moment of her dying.

But Mina's behaviour was in striking contrast to the dramatics enacted by Lady Bartlett and a long line of women before her.

Now, because he was determined to erase the unhappiness from her mind, he deliberately talked of things which interested her most, including the foreign lands he had visited and the sights he had seen in various parts of the world which were connected with history.

He spoke of the Sphinx, the Hanging Gardens of Babylon, and the Taj Mahal, which he thought was one of the most beautiful buildings he had ever seen.

As he was describing it to her he loved the way in which she listened to him with her eyes raised to his, seeming, because she was so interested, almost to hold her breath in case she should miss a word he said.

He told himself that he loved not only the beauty of her face but the beauty of her personality, from which he felt the vibrations more intensely every moment he was with her.

He found himself calculating how long he must wait before he told her of his love, and he knew it was going to be very hard to be with her alone as they had been those past weeks without revealing the intensity of his feelings.

'She is perfect,' he found himself thinking as she gave him a little smile when she was particularly touched by something he had said.

Perhaps because death remained uppermost in their minds, however much they wished to forget it, the conversation turned to the after-life which every religion promises its followers.

They spoke of the Elysian fields of the Greeks, the Valhalla of the Vikings, the Nirvana of the Buddhists, the Garden of Islam of the Moslems, the T'ien of the Chinese, and the sapphire sea and golden harps of the Christian Heaven.

Mina had something to say about them all. Then finally, as if he could not prevent himself from expressing what was in his mind, the Marquis said:

"And of course, for all ordinary men and women, Heaven is really to be with the person one loves."

Without thinking, Mina looked across the Dining-Room to where the portrait of Barbara Castlemaine was hanging on the wall.

She did not speak, but her eyes were very revealing.

"You are intelligent enough to be aware," the Marquis said almost sharply, "that I was speaking of a very different sort of love."

She turned her head to look at him and he went on:

"You have read so much and thought a great deal more, and you know as well as I do that for every man there is a choice between a love which is entirely physical and one which is spiritual, sacred, ideal, and which, although he may not speak of it, is hidden in a sacred shrine in his heart."

Because his voice was deep with sincerity, he saw Mina's eyes widen and after a moment she asked:

"Is . . . that really . . . true?"

"I promise you it is the absolute truth, and although a man may not ever find his ideal woman, he is always searching for her."

He saw that Mina was only half-convinced, and he knew that her thoughts were dwelling on her Stepmother and Eloise Bartlett.

"A man is only human, Mina," the Marquis went on, "and in his journey through life, women are like lovely flowers which decorate his path. Because they are beautiful and fragrant, it is a natural instinct to pick them and make them his. But of course, when like flowers they fade, he discards them."

Mina gave a little sigh and he knew she understood what he was saying to her. He went on:

"But every man longs for a true love, like that of Shah Jehan, who, when the woman he loved more than life itself died, immortalised her in the Taj Mahal. Then he built himself a tomb nearby, so that he could be with her even in death."

He thought the expression in Mina's eyes softened and there was also a radiance about her face, as if the way he spoke made her see the beauty and significance of the Taj Mahal.

Because the Marquis was very experienced where women were concerned, he did not press his argument any further, but went on to talk of other things until they left the Dining-Room, having sat there longer than they usually did, and went into the Drawing-Room,.

While they were talking the stars had come out and the sunset was only a faint glow on the horizon. Behind them the great oak trees filled the Park with mysterious shadows.

Mina walked to the open window and stepped outside onto the terrace to look out over the small lawns and down to the lake.

Her face was turned towards the quiet place where she tried to tame the roe deer and where this morning she had watched the doe die.

The Marquis followed the direction of her eyes and her thoughts, and after a moment he said:

"Because you have been through quite a lot today, Mina, I am going to suggest that you go to bed early. I am planning something very exciting for us to do tomorrow, and I would not wish you to be tired."

She turned to him eagerly, and the light of the stars was in her eyes as she exclaimed:

"Something exciting? What is it?"

"It is a secret," he replied. "If I tell you about it now, you might stay awake, which I would not wish you to do."

"A secret surprise! It sounds very, very exciting!"

"I hope you will think it is," he replied, "but first we must certainly exercise Firefly."

"You know how much I love riding him."

"And he loves you," the Marquis replied, "just as the doves, the birds, and the deer do. You have brought a great deal of love to Vent Royal, Mina."

"That is the nicest compliment I have ever received," she cried, "and thank you for being so kind ... and ... understanding."

There was a little throb in her voice, and he knew she was thinking of the moment when as the doe died she had turned to him instinctively for comfort.

"It is what I hope I may always be," he said quietly. "And now, good-night, Mina."

He bent his head, meaning to kiss her cheek lightly as he would have kissed any child in the same circumstances.

Then somehow, he had no idea how it happened, Mina was looking up at him and she must have moved at the same time.

Instead of her cheek, his lips found hers, and they were just as soft, sweet, and innocent as he had expected they would be.

Because the Marquis had an iron control over himself, and also because he loved Mina in a way he had never loved before, he prevented himself from putting his arms round her.

For the passing of a few seconds—or it may have been a century in time—they were linked together, and he thought that nothing could be more perfect.

Then with a superhuman effort he raised his head.

"Good-night, Mina!" he said, and thought his voice sounded strange and a little unsteady.

For a moment she did not move and her eyes searched his.

Then, as swiftly as the roe deer, she slipped from the terrace into the Drawing-Room and he was alone.

For a moment he was conscious only of the blood throbbing in his temples and the feeling of inexpressible rapture which was moving through his body.

Then he told himself sharply, as if he called himself to order, that she was a child, and that was how he must force himself to think of her for at least another year.

* * *

As she went upstairs to her room, Mina was barely conscious that her feet were moving. All she could think of was the ecstatic wonder of the Marquis's kiss.

When his lips had touched hers, she had felt as if a shaft of sunlight passed between them and evoked a sensation which was unlike anything she had ever imagined or dreamt she could feel.

At the same time, it was utterly perfect, and she knew it could only come from Heaven itself and was the sacred love of which the Marquis had been speaking at dinner.

In all her reading and in her imagination she had never believed that love could make people feel as if they were no longer human but Divine.

In the passing of a second, she had been transformed from herself into Aphrodite, no longer a human being but a goddess.

Now she thought she could understand not only

what the Marquis had tried to explain, but also why she could charm the birds and other animals to her in the same way as her father had done.

It was the vibrations of love that created the "magic" which called them.

That was what she had felt, magnified a million times, when the Marquis's lips had held hers captive.

He had drawn her with his heart, she thought, as she drew the doves, the roe deer, and Firefly.

It was love! Love! Love!

Until now she had not understood that that was the explanation of so much she had never been able to put into words.

She reached her bedroom feeling as if she were walking in the sky rather than on earth, to find that Rose, the maid who had attended her ever since her arrival at Vent Royal, was waiting.

"You're early, Miss."

"Am I?" Mina asked absently.

She had no wish to talk, and somehow it was difficult to understand what was being said to her.

"There's a telegram come for you, Miss," Rose went on. "It only arrived a little while ago, as the post-boy's horse has gone lame and he had to walk up from the village."

She moved across the room, saying as she did so:

"He didn't wait for an answer, not wanting to go back across the Park late at night. He's frightened of seeing ghosties and goblins lurking under the trees, but I tells him there's only the deer."

"A telegram!" Mina murmured almost beneath her breath.

"Yes, Miss. Here it is," Rose said, picking it up from the dressing-table and bringing it to her. "I hopes it's not bad news?"

Mina did not answer. She was opening the telegram with trembling fingers, knowing only too well what she would read, and there was no need for her to see that it came from Italy.

For a moment the words written on the thin paper swam before her eyes. Then she read:

Very, very happy. Important you do immediately exactly as we agreed. Everything Arranged. Love C.H.

Mina read the telegram several times over to make sure she understood exactly what Christine was telling her.

First and most important was that she was married. Her initials confirmed that. Secondly, she was warning her to leave immediately because doubtless she was informing her father that she was Harry's wife, and Harry would at the same time be informing his parents.

'I must go away!' Mina thought in a sudden fright.

She knew she could not bear the questions and reproaches which would certainly be heaped on her by both the Marquis and his grandmother when they knew of her deception.

'I must leave! I must leave at once!' she thought frantically.

"I hope it's not bad news, Miss?" Rose asked.

"I am afraid it is," Mina said, and her voice did not sound like her own. "And, Rose, I want your help."

"Yes, of course, Miss. What can I do?"

"I must leave very early in the morning," Mina answered, "but I do not wish to upset Her Ladyship when she is not well."

"No, of course not, Miss."

"That is why I want you to fetch my trunk and help me pack it."

"Tonight, Miss?"

"Yes, now!" Mina said firmly. "But I do not want anyone else to know what we are doing."

She thought the maid looked curious, and explained:

111

"If Agnes is aware of what is happening, you know she will tell Her Ladyship, and that means she may lie awake worrying about me."

"It's like you, Miss, to be so considerate, and I understands," Rose said.

"Then if you can get the trunk here without there being any commotion about it," Mina said, "and help me to pack it, I will be able to get away first thing tomorrow morning. I will leave a note for Her Ladyship, which can be given to her later in the day."

"I'm sure that'd be best, Miss. But what about His Lordship?"

"I do not wish him to know either," Mina said firmly. "The reason I have to go is a family matter and something I must deal with entirely by myself."

"P'raps it would be wiser if His Lordship's valet tells His Lordship when he calls him."

"No, no!" Mina said quickly. "That is something I have no wish to happen. Promise me, Rose, promise you will say nothing to anybody until after I have gone."

Rose looked at her in a rather bewildered fashion, but, being a good-natured if rather a slow-witted country-girl, she agreed to do what Mina wanted.

"Very well, Miss, if that's what you wants," she said. "I'll get Emily to help me with the trunk. She's the housemaid as sleeps with me."

"Thank you," Mina said, "and please ask Emily to say nothing to anybody."

"Don't you worry yourself, Miss. Emily's as tight as a clam when she wants to be."

Rose hurried away and Mina crossed the room to pull the curtains back from one of the windows.

Outside, the stars filled the sky. She could see their reflection in the lake and they seemed part of the love which still quivered on her lips.

As she looked out into the darkness, Mina was suddenly aware that in leaving Vent Royal she was leaving Heaven.

It was not only the house, the birds, the deer, and the Marchioness who had been so kind to her, it was the Marquis, to whom in some strange, magical way she could not explain she now belonged.

His lips had met hers, and although she might never see him again, she knew, just as he had explained to her at dinner, that he would live forever and for eternity in a shrine in her heart.

"I love him," Mina whispered to the stars.

* * *

Only when the trunks and the hat-box were packed with the clothes that Christine had given her did Mina realise how tired she was.

The elation she had felt on the terrace had gradually ebbed away from her, leaving her depleted of everything but a feeling of weariness which was really one of loss.

When she was alone and had got into bed, she deliberately left the curtains undrawn so that she could still see the stars.

Now as she looked at them through the long window with its diamond-shaped panes, she felt as if they too would be left behind when she went from Vent Royal.

"It is like being thrown out of the Garden of Eden," she told herself, "but when Eve left, Adam went with her, and even in the wilderness they were together."

The she understood what she now realised she had been very foolish not to have understood before.

Why the last two weeks had seemed golden with happiness and why every day had been more exciting than the one before was simply because she had been with the Marquis.

Although she had told herself that she disapproved of him and despised him, she knew that all the time, like a seed germinating in the ground, her love for him had been growing.

113

She had not been aware that it was love, but now she knew she had really fallen in love when he had looked so different from what she had expected, and when as his fingers touched hers a vibration had passed from him to her.

She had forced herself to go on being shocked by his behaviour with Christine's Stepmother and even more shocked by what Lady Bartlett had revealed, but it was all unimportant now beside the fact that she loved him.

Now she could understand, as she had never been able to do before, how a woman would stand by a man and continue to love him whatever crime he might commit.

When she had read of wives who waited for years for their husbands to be freed from prison, or women who had died rather than continue to live without the man they loved, she had thought it was something she would never do herself.

But like a revelation written in fire across the sky she knew that however many women there had been in the Marquis's life, and however reprehensible such liaisons were, she still loved him.

"I would love him if he had committed every crime in the calendar," Mina told the stars.

She felt her whole being reach out to him as if she were sending him the magic thoughts of love which she sent to the birds.

•　•　•

As the stars began to fade, Mina rose and dressed.

"At what time do you rise in the morning?" she had asked Rose.

"We all has to be downstairs by five o'clock, Miss."

"Then as soon as you get downstairs, find a footman and send him to the stables to order a carriage to take me to the station."

"Do you know the time of the train?" Rose enquired.

"There is sure to be one very early in the morning," Mina replied, "and if not, I will wait."

"Surely you'll not be travelling alone, Miss?"

"It is quite all right," Mina answered. "I am only going as far as London."

Rose seemed to accept this explanation even though it was a rather lame one, and Mina knew that she would order the carriage, which was all that mattered.

It would only take about three-quarters-of-an-hour to reach the nearest station, and she reckoned that as the Marquis did not usually reach the stables before seven-thirty, he would not be called before seven o'clock.

If he then learnt of her departure, it would already be too late for him to stop her, even if, as was unlikely, he wished to do so.

When she was dressed, there was still plenty of time to sit down at the desk in her bedroom and write two letters.

The first was for the Marchioness, which Mina worded very carefully in her clear, elegant handwriting:

> *I have to leave, Ma'am, and you will learn later that I am not who I appeared to be, and that I have in fact deceived you.*
>
> *I have no real excuse for doing so, except that I was helping somebody I love.*
>
> *I cannot expect you to forgive me, but I will always think of your kindness with the deepest gratitude, and I shall pray for you always.*
>
> *Mina*

She placed the Marchioness's letter in an envelope and addressed it to her.

Then as she stared down at an empty sheet of

writing-paper, she wondered what she could say to the Marquis.

All she wanted to write were three words: *"I love you!"*

She thought if she did so he would be surprised and perhaps as shocked as she had been when she had learnt about Lady Lydford and Lady Bartlett.

To him she was only a child—a child whom he had taught because of his affection for the woman he thought was her Stepmother.

Mina had no wish to think deeply of what the Marquis felt for Nadine Lydford.

She would hear Christine say that her Stepmother loved him in "a very wild and passionate manner," and Mina knew that her own response to that was jealousy.

She reasoned that his kindness to her and the manner in which he had carried out Lady Lydford's instructions to see that she was educated and looked after arose simply from his deep affection for the woman he loved and who had left him for no other reason than that she had to be with her husband.

Lady Bartlett was different.

The Marquis had grown tired of her, and although she was extremely beautiful, Mina thought no man would care for long for somebody who behaved in such an unrestrained manner.

'It must be Lady Lydford whom he really loves,' she thought, and decided she was glad that she was leaving.

How could she bear to love him as she did now, knowing that his thoughts were centred on somebody else and he was yearning for her?

Because time was passing and she thought that at any moment she might hear a knock on the door when Rose came to collect her trunk, Mina just wrote what came into her mind!

Forgive me, and thank you. I shall never forget.

She did not sign the note, she merely put it quickly into an envelope and left the two letters side-by-side on the desk.

Only as she went down the dark corridor, following the two footmen who were carrying her trunk, did she send her thoughts, because she could not help it, to where the Marquis was sleeping.

"Good-bye," she said, "good-bye. I shall remember you not only for the rest of my life but for eternity."

The same words vibrated from her as she sat waiting in the small wayside station for the train which would carry her to London.

At that early hour of the morning there was only a very old and doddery porter on duty, and the footman from Vent Royal put her trunk in the Guard's-Van and her hat-box beside her in the empty carriage.

Because she knew it would be expected of her, she travelled First-Class, although she worried about the extravagance.

She had tipped Rose generously, and the footman thanked her for what she gave him.

"Sorry to see you leave, Miss," he said. "We hopes you'll be back soon."

"You have all been very kind to me," Mina replied.

The shrill shriek of the Guard's whistle made the footman shut the carriage door hastily, and as the train moved slowly off he waved and Mina waved back to him.

She felt as though he was her last glimpse of Vent Royal and now she had lost it forever.

Then as the train gathered speed she told herself that she had to think what she must do.

She had already decided that she would not go to Rome, for the time being at any rate.

She was quite sure that Christine was asking her to join them only out of kindness, for now that she and Harry were married they would not really want anybody else with them.

117

Mina could remember her mother saying how happy she had been with her father when instead of going on an expensive honeymoon they had settled straight way into the small Manor House which was to be their home for the rest of their married life together.

"We were alone," she had told Mina, "completely alone at first, until we could find suitable servants, and there were only two old women from the village who came in to clean the house."

There was a smile on her lips as she reminisced.

"That is what made it so wonderful—to be alone with your father. My father and mother were so strict about the proprieties that we had hardly been permitted to talk to each other alone for any length of time."

"Did it not seem rather strange?" Mina asked.

"Not strange," her mother answered, "but marvellous and very exciting."

There was a softness in her voice and the expression in her eyes said more than words, and Mina thought that being alone with the Marquis as much as she had been at Vent Royal had been very much the same.

'It was love which made every day seem more golden with sunshine than the last,' she thought, 'and it was love that made me want him to think I was intelligent.'

She thought back over the conversations they had had, how much she had learnt, and how exciting it had been to talk with a man on subjects which had interested them both.

"At least they interested me," Mina told herself, and wondered if the Marquis had been pretending.

"Perhaps really I seemed rather ignorant and a bore to him," she reflected humbly.

But she was certain that if he had been bored he would have gone back to London.

She was well aware that his grandmother was surprised that he had stayed for so long and had teased him about it when he and Mina were with her in her Sitting-Room.

"I cannot think what they are doing in London without you, Tian," she had said.

"I expect they are managing, Grandmama," the Marquis replied.

"The gossips of St. James's will have nothing to talk about, and you will certainly be missed at all the Balls, and perhaps your lady-friend will have found somebody else to take your place."

"I have always been told that 'absence makes the heart grow fonder,'" the Marquis parried.

"I still think that when you do return, you will find the flags at half-mast," the Marchioness said mockingly.

When she was alone with Mina, the Marchioness had told her how efficiently the Marquis ran the Estate.

"Even though he is away a great deal," she said, "he still keeps his finger on the pulse, and in some way peculiarly his own, he knows exactly what is happening! Woe betide any of his employees who neglect his instructions!"

"I am sure that is true," Mina had replied. "I never imagined that any place as big as this could be so perfect in every particular."

"That is what my husband always aimed for—perfection," the Marchioness said, "and if he was alive today, I know he would be proud of his grandson."

"As you are, Ma'am."

"Yes, I am," the Marchioness agreed. "At the same time, I wish he would marry and settle down. I would like to see my great-grandson before I die."

"I am sure you will do that, Ma'am," Mina answered with a little smile. "There is no reason to think of you dying for years and years."

At the same time, when she was alone and thought over the conversation, she found herself wondering what the Marquis's wife would be like.

Since he was in love with Lady Lydford and the

plan for him to marry her stepdaughter had been, unknown to him, ruined, it certainly did not seem likely that he would immediately start all over again to find somebody suitable.

"There must be hundreds of girls who would fill the bill," Mina told herself, and found the thought strangely depressing.

If the Marquis was annoyed by her deception, and she was quite certain that he would be, she could not help feeling that Lady Lydford would be absolutely furious.

There was nothing she could do directly to Christine, since she was now protected by Harry and also had her own money, but, Mina thought with a little stab of fear, perhaps she would punish her in some way or another.

"There is nothing she can do to me," she told herself reassuringly.

Yet at the same time it was frightening to think that she was alone in the world and if there was any real unpleasantness there was nobody to whom she could turn for help.

"The best thing I can do is to disappear," she told herself.

That meant not travelling to Italy to meet Christine, but going home.

The idea came to her almost like a ray of light.

Of course that was what she would do.

Instead of trying to find employment or returning to Mrs. Fontwell, which she felt she would rather die than do, she would go back to the house which held all the memories of her father and mother and her childhood.

If the house had been closed, somebody in the village would have the key, and because they had known her all her life, they would not prevent her from camping out in the Manor until she had thought out her future.

"I must think! I have to think!" Mina told herself.

She had enough money to enable her to live carefully, besides the cheque that Christine had given her.

The one hundred pounds was meant for her fare to Italy, but she knew that in an emergency she could borrow a little of it until she could find some way of earning money.

When she thought about it, she knew it was going to be very hard to find someone as kind to her as the Marchioness had been, and there would never be anybody like the Marquis.

Knowing that she would never see him again gave her a feeling as if she carried a stone in her chest, and it seemed to prevent her from breathing.

She knew it was despair, dismay, and unhappiness at losing him, all rolled into one, which made her feel like that.

Then as the train drew nearer to London she told herself that she was no longer a child either in reality or in pretence and she had to grow up and behave in an adult fashion.

It was this newfound resolution and determination which enabled her to collect her luggage in quite an efficient manner, change stations, and find herself another train to carry her to Lincolnshire.

It might have taken away some of her confidence if she had realised that the main reason why everything went so smoothly was that she looked too young and far too pretty to be travelling alone.

Porters looked after her in a fatherly manner, the driver of the hackney-carriage took every care to take her to the right entrance to the station, and the Guard of the train leaving London enquired if she was all right before he actually signalled the train to start.

However, even with such assistance, it was a long journey and a difficult one, for she had another change to make before she reached the station nearest to her home.

However, there was a Carrier in the little market-town which she finally reached later in the afternoon.

Mina asked for him at the station and learnt that he would be collecting a number of parcels at any time in the next hour.

Feeling that fortune was smiling on her, she waited, and when he arrived he was delighted to drive her the five miles home.

Being very well informed about the small villages he served, he was able to tell her to whom her uncle had entrusted the care of the house and who had the key.

"'T be Mrs. Briggs, Miss Mina," he said. "Ye remembers 'er?"

"Yes, of course I remember Mrs. Briggs!" Mina exclaimed. "She was very fond of Mama and Papa, so I am sure she will let me stay at home until I can find employment of some sort."

"Oi 'ears as how ye weren't left much money," the Carrier said. "'Twere a shame, as yer father were a fine gent'man."

Mina felt warmed by the sincerity in his voice, and he talked about her father and mother as the horse plodded down the dusty lanes, eager to be back in his comfortable stall.

When they reached the Manor, the Carrier said:

"Oi'll take ye up 't the front door, and ye can put yer trunk down there. Then Oi'll go an' tell Mrs. Briggs ye're 'ere. There'll be no need for ye to come wi' Oi."

"Thank you for being so very kind to me," Mina said.

Because once again she looked so small and pathetic outside the locked front door and the boarded-up windows, the Carrier refused to take any payment for the journey.

"Ye keep yer money, Miss," he said. "'T dunna last forever!"

He drove away and Mina sat down forlornly on her trunk until the sound of the wheels could no longer be heard.

Then as the joy and comfort of being home

enfolded her, she found herself thinking once again of the Marquis.

Instead of the small gabled Manor House, weather-worn from the winds blowing over the fens and the front door badly in need of a coat of paint, she could see only the magnificence and beauty of Vent Royal.

The gleaming gold of the setting sun shone on its windows, the Marquis's standard fluttered in the evening breeze, and a flight of white pigeons moved over the flower-filled gardens towards their dove-cots.

'The birds of Aphrodite,' Mina thought to herself.

Once again she felt the Marquis's lips on hers, and her heart flew back to him on wings.

Chapter Seven

The Marquis walked into White's in a bad temper.

He had spent a difficult and frustrating morning trying to get some sense out of the caretakers at Lydford House.

They had seemed to him to be completely half-witted, and he had not obtained a single coherent answer to his questions.

They could not remember when they had last seen Miss Christine; they did not know where she went to School; they thought Lord Lydford's secretary was on holiday; they could not remember the names of the servants who had gone to the country.

After nearly an hour of questioning, the Marquis extracted from the woman, who seemed a little brighter than her husband, that a young lady whom she had never seen before had come to the house one morning about three weeks ago and had left almost immediately in another carriage.

He had learnt no more, for although the Marquis was sure that it must have been Mina, the woman could not give a recognisable description of her.

The Marquis, like his grandmother, had been astounded, then bewildered by the contents of the letters which Mina had left for them.

When he had risen as usual at seven o'clock and gone to the stables, he had expected to find Mina there before him.

As he walked over the cobbled yard, he thought

he would hear her soft voice talking to Firefly and he felt as eager to see her as any young boy with his first love.

He knew she would turn her head at his approach with a light in her eyes and a faint smile on her lips.

As he thought of the lips he had kissed last night, the Marquis felt his heart beating quicker and there was an excitement rising within him that was different from anything he had known in the past.

It was not all a physical sensation but something very much more subtle, an emotion which his determination to control himself had lifted into the realms of chivalry.

In fact, in his desire to protect Mina even from himself, he felt that he dedicated himself to her service like any Knight entering a joust with her favour carried on his helmet.

'I love her!' he thought. 'And our lives together will be a story of devotion and happiness which will certainly surprise those who criticise me.'

He reached the stable-door and with a decided throb of disappointment found that Mina was not there.

"Where is Miss Lydford?" he asked Abbey, who was saddling the stallion which he had said he would ride this morning.

"She be late, M'Lord," Abbey replied, "an' it's unlike 'er not to be 'ere afore Your Lordship."

"It is indeed," the Marquis agreed.

Five minutes later he sent one of the grooms running to the house to enquire what was keeping Miss Lydford from joining him.

For the first time he wondered if she felt embarrassed after what had happened last night.

At the time he had known with a sure sensitivity that she had been swept as he had been up to the stars by a rapture that neither of them could deny.

The Marquis was far too experienced not to

realise that she had responded to him, and it was he and not she who had ended the wonder of their kiss.

He could not believe in retrospect that she had regretted what had happened or was too frightened to meet him again. At the same time, he could not be certain of anything, except that Mina was not there and the horses were waiting.

Abbey and another groom brought them out into the yard and the Marquis stood beside them, not speaking but tapping his highly polished boot with his riding-whip.

The groom he had sent to the house came running back, but there was no sign of Mina, and the Marquis with a frown between his eyes waited for an explanation.

The groom was breathless as he reached his side.

"They says, M'Lord, Miss Lydford b'aint there."

"What do you mean—she is not there?" the Marquis asked sharply.

"Er left early this morning, M'Lord."

The Marquis stared at the groom incredulously.

Then as he realised that the lad would be unable to answer the questions he wished to ask, he strode off towards the house, leaving Abbey looking after him in a worried manner.

The footmen in the Hall were sent flying in every direction to find the Butler, who was not usually in attendance at such an early hour, and the Housekeeper was fetched while having her breakfast and was obviously flustered by the questions which the Marquis barked at her.

"What time did Miss Lydford leave?" he enquired. "And why was I not informed?"

"I've only just learnt of it myself, M'Lord," the Housekeeper replied. "It seems Miss Lydford asked to be taken to the station as early as five o'clock this morning."

"Did she give any explanation?"

"She received a telegram last night which Rose thought contained bad news."

"A telegram? What telegram?" the Marquis asked.

It took some time to ascertain that the telegram had been brought to the house very late because the post-boy's horse was lame, and Rose had taken it up to Mina's bedroom. This meant, the Marquis knew, that she had received it after she left him.

Rose was sent for, and she related nervously how Mina had asked for her trunk but told her to say nothing to anybody else in case it should upset the Marchioness.

"Miss Mina left a note for Her Ladyship which she said'd explain everything," she finished.

"A note?" the Marquis almost shouted.

"An' one for Your Lordship," Rose faltered.

"Then why have I not been given it?" he demanded.

It appeared that Rose had given the note addressed to the Marchioness to Agnes so that she could receive it later in the morning when she was called.

The note for the Marquis she had given to one of the footmen, who had taken it to the Pantry, where it was waiting until the Butler should carry it through on a silver salver to the front of the house for the Marquis to receive when he returned from riding.

By the time the Marquis had untangled the channels of communication which existed amongst his staff, the Butler had brought the note inscribed with his name.

He took it from the salver and walked into the Library to read it alone.

What he read left him no wiser and in a fever of curiosity. He knew, however, that he must wait for an hour until his grandmother was called at nine o'clock.

For a long time he just stared at Mina's handwriting, and the words *I shall never forget* seemed to spring out at him from the paper in a way which not only disturbed but also frightened him.

He could not imagine what he had to forgive, but that she would never forget what had happened at Vent Royal suggested that she did not mean to return and was in fact saying good-bye.

Finally, because he could not bear to be inactive, the Marquis sent for Firefly to be brought round to the front door and rode off into the Park.

As if Firefly sensed that he was upset, and perhaps being also disappointed that Mina was not riding him, he played up in the most outrageous fashion.

This at least kept the Marquis from brooding, since he had to concentrate on preventing the horse from bucking him off or rearing at every leaf or shadow which crossed their path.

Finally Firefly acknowledged that the Marquis was the master, and they galloped until the Marquis thought it was nearing the time when he could see his grandmother and turned for home.

Because the Marchioness was very particular about how she appeared, the Marquis had to wait until nearly half-after-nine before she would admit him to her bedroom.

By then she had opened Mina's note, which Agnes had given her, and as the Marquis came through the door she asked:

"What has happened? Where has Mina gone? And how can she say that she was deceiving us?"

"I have been waiting, Grandmama," the Marquis said, "until I could see what she had written to you. The note she left for me consists of only a few words."

The Marquis reached the bedside and the Marchioness held Mina's letter out to him.

He took it and read what she had written, and when he reached the end he read it again.

As he did so, the Marchioness watched his face as if from what she saw she might learn something which would give her an explanation of what had happened.

"*I am not who I appeared to be,*'" the Marquis

quoted as if he spoke to himself, " *'and I have in fact deceived you.'* What can she mean by that?"

"Agnes told me that she received a telegram last night."

"Yes, I have been told that too," the Marquis said, "but she did not leave it behind her, so we have no idea what was in it."

"Then if she was not Christine Lydford, as this note appears to suggest," the Marchioness said, "who was she?"

"I have not the slightest idea," the Marquis replied. "Nadine said she was sending her to me, and when she arrived I did not question for a moment that she was not Lydford's daughter."

"I do not understand," the Marchioness said. "She was so sweet that I would have been prepared to swear that every word she spoke and every thought in her head was honest and true."

The Marquis did not reply and after a moment his grandmother said:

"I loved her. She was one of the most adorable creatures I have ever met in the whole of my life, and I thought sometimes that she belonged to me and was the granddaughter I have always longed for."

The Marquis walked to the window to stand looking out at the white doves on the lawn below.

He could see Mina holding up her outstretched arms as she had done that morning when he had found her in the water-lily garden.

It was something she had done many times since, but he thought that the first time he had seen her showing her amazing power over the birds and especially the doves she had looked like Aphrodite herself.

He had known in that moment that she symbolised the love that was the ideal emotion he had sought.

He knew that amongst the doves sitting on top of the dove-cot or clustered on the grass was the one whose leg she had set with a splint, and which had since joined the others, none the worse for his injury.

Could anyone who could evoke, just by being herself, the trust of birds and animals be anything but as pure and perfect as he believed her to be?

Yet she had written: "*I have in fact deceived you.*"

"It is obvious to me," the Marchioness said behind him, "that the person Mina was helping must be Christine Lydford."

The Marquis looked down again at the letter which he still held in his hand, and read: "*I have no real excuse except that I was helping somebody I love.*"

"Yes, of course, that must be the explanation," he said, a note of relief in his voice.

He had barely been able to express it to himself, but when he read the words: "*somebody I love,*" he had had a sudden fear and an irrepressible jealousy that it might be a man.

He went back to his grandmother's side.

"What you are thinking, Grandmama," he said, "is that Mina took Christine's place here so that she could help her. But why? And how? And if that is true, then where is Christine?"

"I can only imagine," the Marchioness said, "that she did not agree to her Stepmother's plan of sending her here."

That was something that had never occurred to the Marquis, and as he looked at the Marchioness in surprise, she went on:

"Girls of that age have very strong opinions of their own, and I am quite sure that Christine was not consulted but was merely informed that her Stepmother had arranged for her to come to Vent Royal to finish her education, and to leave School, where, for all we know, she was very happy."

As the Marchioness spoke, it struck the Marquis for the first time that perhaps Nadine Lydford had been indiscreet or "cold-blooded" enough to tell her

Stepdaughter what plans she had actually made.

If she had, then Christine might well have had very decided objections to marrying a man she had never seen and certainly not one chosen for her by her Stepmother.

As he thought about it, he knew he had been a fool. He had accepted the arrangements that had been made with such speed by Nadine Lydford because it had seemed too late for him to do anything about it.

He had therefore sent his carriage to London, as she had requested, to pick up a girl who would already have left her School before he had received his own instructions.

Now he realised that the whole idea which had sprung from Nadine's fertile imagination would be an insult to any girl who was sensitive and doubtless romantic.

Just as he was perceptive enough to realise that Nadine resented her Stepdaughter, he suspected that Christine would undoubtedly resent the woman who had taken her mother's place.

"How could I have been so blind?" the Marquis asked himself.

He could understand now why Mina when he first saw her had looked at him fearfully, then with a contempt that had surprised him.

He remembered how she had stiffened when he had spoken unthinkingly and stupidly about it, and she had connected Barbara Castlemaine's position as the mistress of Charles II with Nadine Lydford's position with him.

'I should have realised then that no girl with any decent feelings would wish to marry her Stepmother's lover,' the Marquis thought.

Then with a sudden feeling of joy that was almost like a light at the end of a dark passage he realised that at least that did not apply to Mina.

If she was not Nadine Lydford's Stepdaughter, then that was one barrier that was not erected between them.

"What I think you must do," the Marchioness was saying as he stood silent and reflective by her bedside, "is to find Mina."

"But of course, Grandmama. That is what I mean to do."

"I have a feeling there is something very strange about her leaving us hurriedly and without saying good-bye. I know she was fond of me, and no-one, however well they acted, could have pretended the happiness that radiated from her because she loved this house and the birds, the doves, and of course your horses."

"I agree with you," the Marquis said in a low voice. "They unmistakably all made her very, very happy."

The Marchioness was about to add something else, then thought it would be a mistake to say what was in her mind.

Instead she put out her hand towards her grandson, saying:

"Find her, Tian. Find her for me, if for nobody else. I cannot bear to lose her."

The Marquis raised her hand to his lips.

"I will find her and bring her back to you," he promised, and she knew it was a vow which he would keep.

* * *

As the Marquis travelled to London, knowing that he must begin his search at Lydford House, he read and reread the letter Mina had written to the Marchioness, hoping it would give him some clue as to where she had gone and who she actually was.

He had thought that the first stage of his search would be comparatively easy.

But when he left Lydford House he knew that he was no wiser than he had been on arrival, and he began to feel afraid.

The next step was obvious: to discover where

Christine Lydford had been at School, and that meant a journey to Lydford House in Buckinghamshire.

He could imagine the commotion his sudden appearance would cause amongst the servants, and the gossip he would arouse not only amongst Lord Lydford's staff, but doubtless in the vicinity.

He was not so foolish as not to know that Nadine's servants, especially those who had been in London until she left for India, must have been well aware of the way their mistress was behaving with him in her husband's absence.

If he now began making enquiries about the disappearance of her Stepdaughter, it would seem peculiar to say the least of it.

It must certainly cause a spate of speculation which would ripple out to other houses in the neighbourhood, and more than likely in the usual manner of such chattering it would eventually reach London.

For the first time in his long, raffish career as a Rake, the Marquis felt embarrassed and censorious of his own behaviour.

He knew because he loved Mina that he was not prepared to shrug his shoulders and ignore what people might say about her.

He could not bear to think that she might be hurt by what was said, or, worse still, that she might be ashamed.

Because he loved her, he wanted everything round her to be beautiful and perfect. He did not want her to be touched by the ugliness of a passion that had nothing spiritual or sacred about it, and most of all he wanted her to admire him as a man.

If he was unable to find out at Lydford House what had happened to her, what should he do?

It was a question he kept asking himself over and over again as he went into White's Club.

It was luncheon-time, and as the Bar, which was not very big, appeared to be crowded, the Marquis decided he would go straight into the Dining-Room.

He walked across the room with its windows overlooking St. James's Street, nodding to several friends who waved to him as he passed them without stopping to sit down at a table laid for two at the far end.

A waiter hurried to his side, and he ordered without much interest, barely glancing at the wine-list and choosing the first claret he happened to see.

He was aroused from his reverie, which had made him unaware of his surroundings, to find that there was somebody standing at his table.

He looked up to see Lord Hawkstone, whom, as an older man, he did not number among his close friends but whom he met frequently.

They were both members of the Jockey Club and of White's, and Lord Hawkstone, whose horses he continually beat on the race-course, was always good-humoured enough to congratulate him unreservedly.

As the Marquis looked up at him, he thought in surprise that Lord Hawkstone appeared somewhat embarrassed.

"I suppose I should apologise to you, Ventnor," he said before the Marquis could speak, "but at the same time you must admit that it is not often I get the opportunity to pip you at the post, so to speak."

The Marquis raised his eye-brows.

He was wondering what Lord Hawkstone was referring to, since his own horses had not participated in any race-meetings during the last two weeks.

"I only received the letter from my son this morning," Lord Hawkstone went on. "It explained to me very frankly the whole situation, but I found it hard to believe that you were in fact a party to it."

What he was saying left the Marquis no wiser than he had been at the beginning of the conversation, and after a moment he said:

"I have only just arrived from the country, and you have me somewhat at a disadvantage. I have no idea to what you are referring."

Now Lord Hawkstone looked even more embarrassed.

"Do you mean to say you do not know what I am talking about?" he asked. "I thought from what Harry wrote to me that you would be aware by now that it was not Christine Lydford who was with you at Vent Royal."

The Marquis started and his attitude changed.

"Now I understand what you are talking about," he said sharply. "It is something which is of extreme interest to me, so I would be obliged, My Lord, if you would sit down and tell me exactly what you know of this matter."

The Marquis spoke in such an authoritative tone that Lord Hawkstone was taken aback.

Then, as if he felt he had embroiled himself in something that would have been better left alone, he looked towards the other end of the Dining-Room, as if he contemplated beating a retreat.

The Marquis sensed what was in his mind and said quickly:

"I beg you to explain what has happened, since I am completely at sea in the matter, and so is my grandmother."

With some reluctance Lord Hawkstone sat down in the seat opposite the Marquis.

"I felt certain that you would know as much as I do," he said unhappily.

"Suppose we pool our knowledge," the Marquis suggested, "and you tell me first what you have heard from your son."

"I do not know if you have met Harry, my second son," Lord Hawkstone replied, "but I have had a letter form him this morning from Rome, telling me that he has married Christine Lydford, who as you know is Lady Lydford's Stepdaughter."

As he spoke, he glanced at the Marquis in a way which showed that he was well aware of the part Nadine had played in his life before she had left for India.

Then he went on quickly:

"The girl will not be seventeen for another month, so it is a somewhat unusual marriage. But in her father's absence her uncle gave his consent, and Harry informs me that they have loved each other for a long time."

"What else did he say?" the Marquis asked.

While Lord Hawkstone was speaking he had signalled to the waiter to pour him out a glass of claret from the bottle standing beside him, and, as if he thought he needed it, Lord Hawkstone took a quick drink before he said, not looking at the Marquis:

"Harry told me it was Lady Lydford's idea that Christine should stay with you for a year and that when her education was complete you would be married, which of course explains his somewhat precipitate action in making sure that that was an impossibility."

Lord Hawkstone took another drink, and, as there was still silence from the man opposite, he added:

"I am not going to pretend to you, Ventnor, that I am not pleased by the marriage. Christine Lydford is a very wealthy young woman and I cannot afford to give Harry, as my second son, anything but a small allowance. But if they are as happy as my son says they are, then it is certainly an ideal arrangement from my point of view."

The Marquis found his voice.

"When you write to your son, My Lord, will you give him my congratulations and tell him that as far as I am concerned, I think he did exactly the right thing!"

As if the Marquis's approval took a weight off Lord Hawkstone's shoulders, he leant back in his chair to say:

"That is damned generous of you, Ventnor, and I am greatly relieved that you are taking it like a sportsman."

"There is one thing I want to know," the Marquis said. "Did your son say in the letter who had taken Christine's place?"

Lord Hawkstone smiled.

"Harry said it was Christine's idea to play for time to preclude any chance that Lydford or his wife should somehow prevent their marriage from taking place."

"Who was it who came to Vent Royal in Christine's place?" the Marquis asked.

There was a note of urgency as well as of eagerness in his voice, which surprised Lord Hawkstone.

"Now let me see," he said. "I think Harry did tell me who she was, and I have his letter with me."

He started to search through his pockets and the Marquis held his breath.

Finally the letter was discovered in an inside pocket of his coat.

There was further delay while Lord Hawkstone searched for his spectacles, and with difficulty the Marquis prevented himself from snatching up the closely written sheets of paper which he had put down on the table in front of him.

At last, with his spectacles on his nose, he read very slowly through sheet after sheet of his son's letter until he found what he sought.

"Ah, here it is!" he said, and read aloud:

"As you can imagine, we were extremely apprehensive, although we were very ably chaperoned by Christine's maid, who has been with her since she was a baby, in case anyone should suspect that we were eloping and where we were going. Lord Lydford might have been informed, and a telegram from him could have resulted in our being stopped at the last moment from becoming man and wife.

It was Christine's idea to send someone in her place to Vent Royal, pretending to be her, and she found a School-friend who was willing to help us.

137

We are sending her a telegram to join us in Rome after we calculate that you will have received this letter, and Christine left her enough money for the journey. But if by any chance things go wrong and she is troubled over what she has done, it would be kind of you, Papa, if you would do what you could to help her.

Mina's father is dead and so is her mother, Christine tells me she has no money, and her home where she lived in Lincolnshire has been closed by her uncle, Colonel Osbert Shaldon, whom I daresay you know as he was in the Grenadiers.

Anyway, we are extremely grateful to Mina Shaldon for helping us, and when she joins us we will do our best to show our gratitude by giving her a good time."

Lord Hawkstone put down the letter.

"That is all he says about the girl," he said. "The rest is apologising to me and my wife and telling us how much we will like Christine when we meet her. There is no doubt that the boy is head-over-heels in love."

The Marquis had found out what he wanted to know.

"Thank you," he said quietly.

Lord Hawkstone emptied his glass and rose from the table.

"I have a guest waiting for me in the Bar," he said. "I am extremely relieved, Ventnor, that you have taken this, as I might have expected, in the same sporting manner which you take your failures on the race-course."

He smiled before he added:

"Not that you have many!"

The Marquis smiled in return, and when Lord Hawkstone had left him he ate his luncheon with an appetite that he had lost ever since finding that Mina had left Vent Royal.

* * *

Mina walked from the Dining-Room, having eaten the egg that Mrs. Briggs had cooked for her and drunk a cup of tea which was much too strong but was just as Mrs. Briggs herself liked it.

However, she had barely been conscious of what she was eating, for her thoughts were far away at Vent Royal as they had been ever since she had returned home.

She found it difficult not to compare the worn, thread-bare carpets in the Manor, the faded curtains, and the dusty and unpolished furniture with the beauty and luxury that pervaded the house which, as usual, she was thinking of as a special Paradise.

But at least if the Manor did not measure up to the loveliness that was so appropriate a background for the Marquis, the birds which had been part of her life ever since she was a baby were still outside.

At this time of the year there would be ducks nesting on the fens and the tide would be gurgling in the crab-holes, the wind running through the sea-lavender and the saltings.

Hundreds of widgeons would be feeding out on the muds that inch by inch would be disappearing as the tide came in.

She had not far to go before she could see the sea-flats where the geese fed under the moon, where she had watched with her father the great grey birds flighting in from the Arctic.

But there was no need to leave the garden to find the small birds which, if they were not the same, would be the descendants of those who had grown up beside her.

They trusted her as their fathers and grandfathers had done and perhaps, for all she knew, their great-grandfathers.

There would be young blackbirds and wagtails, chaffinches and robins, the wrens which she had told the Marquis she resembled, the tits, the swallows, and perhaps, if she was fortunate, a nut-hatch or a hedge-warbler.

When they were disturbed, as they would be at her appearance until they realised who she was, they would begin to sing loudly, just as sometimes they would sing all night.

As Mina walked into the garden, which was even wilder and more unkept than it had been before she went away, she thought that now that it was summer, the nightingales would have returned from the Continent and perhaps tonight she would hear them sing.

In the past as her father had taught her she would listen for them, and sometimes they would go out together in the moonlight and she would hear them making love to each other as they perched on the trees nearby.

Thinking of love made her remember the Marquis, and for the moment the birds were forgotten and all that she could think about was him.

She had wandered towards a piece of rising ground from which, if she climbed to the top of it, she could see the sea in the distance, blue under a clear sky.

She and her father had called it the look-out, but it was also a place where Mina would go when she was upset or perturbed and wished to be alone.

Now as she moved over the long grass bright with buttercups, cuckoo-flowers, and red poppies, she told herself that she had come home. But the comforting feeling she had expected of being where she belonged was missing.

She reached the look-out and found that the view was just as exquisite as she had remembered it.

She sat down with her back against a silver birch whose leaves protected her from the sun, to see the water gleaming amongst the green where the Vikings had once landed, and to smell the salt of the sea combined with the scent of the reeds and the flowers in the grass.

She sat very still and could hear the birds in the trees above her and wondered if she should call them to her.

Then when she would have done so she found instead that she was sending out her magic not to the birds but towards the Marquis.

It was impossible to think of anything else but his handsome face, to hear anything but his deep voice, while the sea became the grey of his eyes and the wind the touch of his lips.

"I love him! I love him!"

She said it in her heart and her lips moved as if to the music of the gods.

Then she heard a slight movement and looked up to find the Marquis standing beside her.

For a moment she thought she must be dreaming.

Then without speaking he sat down on the grass, facing her in the same way as he had in the Park when he had found her trying to tame the roe deer.

Mina's eyes were held by his and it was impossible to think of anything else; to ask how he had found her and why he was there; or to be aware of anything except him.

It was as if she had called him with her magic and it had not failed her.

The Marquis looked at her as if he had never seen her before, his eyes on the child-like oval of her face, the line of her little straight nose, the softness of her lips.

Then he looked into the blue of her eyes which had a depth in them which he knew was not only part of her beauty but of her intelligence and her character.

"The only time I have ever known you to do a cruel thing," he said at last in a voice that did not sound like his own, "was when you left without telling me where you were going."

As if she suddenly realised why she had left, Mina looked away from him and the colour rose in her cheeks as she said:

"I had to go when I ... learnt that ... Christine was married."

"I can understand that, but I thought, because

141

you seemed so happy at Vent Royal and have given us so much love, that you would understand how deeply hurt and distressed we would be at losing you."

Mina gave a little cry.

"I did not . . . mean to do that . . . I thought you would be . . . angry because I had . . . deceived you."

"I am angry only because you left as you did."

"I . . . am sorry . . . truly . . . sorry," Mina said, "but . . . I could not . . . bear to explain to your grandmother, or to you, what I had . . . done."

"You minded what I would feel or think?"

The colour deepened in Mina's cheeks and he knew she was finding it difficult to know what she should say.

"I understand from Lord Hawkstone that your friend Christine is expecting you to join her in Italy."

Mina glanced at the Marquis and he knew she was realising how he had learnt what had happened and who she was.

He did not speak, and after a moment she said slowly:

"I thought . . . as Christine and Harry were so happy on their . . . honeymoon that they would not . . . want anybody with them."

"Using my instinct and my perception as you have taught me to do," the Marquis said softly, "I was certain you would feel like that and therefore come home."

"There was . . . nowhere else I . . . could go."

"Which made it easier for me to find you."

She gave him a questioning little glance but did not put it into words, and after a moment the Marquis said:

"It was very wrong of you to be so selfish as to leave everybody so upset. My grandmother was in tears. Firefly was behaving atrociously yesterday when I left and he had almost kicked his stall down! And I am quite certain the roe deer and the birds think you have deserted them."

Mina clasped her hands together in an impulsive little gesture.

"It . . . it may have seemed . . . wrong to do what I did . . . but I could not tell you that I had . . . lied to you."

"So you minded what I would think?"

"Of . . . course I . . . minded!"

"Tell me why."

There was silence. Then she said:

"You had been . . . so kind."

"Is that all?"

"N-no . . . there is—was much . . . more. You . . . talked to me . . . taught me . . . let me . . . ride your horses, and . . ."

She stopped, and after a moment the Marquis said very softly:

"And—I kissed you, Mina."

He saw the flush that rose from her throat to her eyes and he said:

"It was the most perfect and marvellous kiss I have ever known in my whole life."

Slowly, very slowly it seemed to him, as if she was drawn irresistibly to do so, Mina turned her head towards him and their eyes met.

"I love you! You must realise that by this time," he said.

She drew in her breath in an audible little gasp, and he went on:

"I want you to tell me what you feel for me."

Now she could look at him no longer, and her eye-lashes were dark and long against her cheeks.

"Tell me!" he insisted.

He knew she was trembling, and in a swift movement he came nearer to her to put his arms round her, and as he did so she turned her face to hide it against his shoulder.

He held her very closely as he had done after the doe died, and with his lips on her hair he said:

"I am waiting."

"I . . . love . . . you! I love you so much that it has been agonising to . . . go away and . . . l-leave you."

The Marquis's arms tightened. Then he asked, still very quietly:

"How old are you?"

"I am eighteen."

For a moment the Marquis was still, as if he could not comprehend the wonder of what he had hoped, and yet feared he might be mistaken.

Then he gave an exclamation of joy and triumph, and to Mina it was like the sound of her birds as he turned her face up to his.

He looked down at her, with her eyes shy but with an indescribable light in them, her mouth trembling a little, yet filled too with the ecstasy of anticipation because she knew he was going to kiss her.

"I love you!" he said. "I love you until it is impossible to think of anything else but you. I cannot live without you!"

Then his lips were on hers.

To Mina it was as if there was a blazing light which came from the sky and enveloped them with a beauty that was also part of their hearts and souls.

It was so rapturous, so utterly and completely glorious, that for a moment she felt as if she must have died and found Heaven, where she and the Marquis were alone except for the glory of God Himself.

Then as the Marquis kissed her and went on kissing her, she felt as if he drew her closer and closer until she was no longer herself but a part of him and they were one.

She could hear the birds singing a paean of praise above them, and the magic of the fens became the magic of Vent Royal.

The whole world whirled round her. Then there was nothing else but the arms, the lips, and the closeness of a man to whom she had belonged in eternities past and would belong for eternities to come.

When finally the Marquis raised his head, they were both transfigured by the intensity of their feelings and the wonder they had found together.

The Marquis looked at her for a long time, then he put out his hand to touch her cheek.

"I love you and worship you!" His voice was deep and unsteady. "How soon will you marry me, my darling?"

"I feel as . . . if we were . . . married already," Mina whispered.

"That is exactly what I want you to say," he answered. "Oh, my precious, has there ever been anybody like you? But how could there be? You are mine—my heart, my soul, my mind, in fact part of my whole being—and without you I am incomplete, as I have been in the past."

"I think you have always been in my dreams . . . in everything I have . . . imagined and thought beautiful and . . . perfect."

She made an inarticulate little sound as she added:

"I have been . . . calling to you ever since I left . . . Vent Royal. It was impossible to do . . . anything else."

"I heard you," the Marquis said, "and I was calling to you, but I was desperately, horribly afraid in case I should not find you."

She knew from the way he spoke that it had been a very real fear, and she said:

"I think perhaps I would have been . . . forced to come back to you . . . as the birds come homing . . . however far they have been away in strange continents . . . and empty deserts . . . they always come . . . home."

The Marquis's arms tightened.

"I will not risk it! You will stay with me and be with me from this moment and forever more!"

Then as if the idea of losing her frightened him, he bent his head and kissed her fiercely, passionately, demandingly, in a very different manner from the way he had kissed her before.

She felt the fire on his lips and felt a strange flame flicker within herself and rise to meet it.

She knew that this was another side to love, different from the sacredness of his first kiss, and yet it was still love.

The love which was perfect and which happened when a man and woman found the ideal for which they had searched and which lay in a sacred shrine within themselves.

* * *

A long time later, when she was still close in the Marquis's arms and the sun was dazzling on the still water of the fens, Mina said:

"You must be ... hungry. Shall we go ... back to the ... house? I will try to ... find you something to eat."

"It is a long time since I had breakfast," the Marquis answered. "I came as far as Stamford last night and stayed at an Hotel because I did not wish to frighten you, if you were here, by appearing very late."

"I wish I had ... known you were ... near me," Mina said. "I lay awake thinking of you and looking at the stars as we ... looked at them ... before you ... kissed me."

"It was something I had not meant to do, because I thought you were a child," the Marquis explained. "But I knew when my lips touched yours that whatever your age might be, you were a woman, my precious, and as a woman you belonged to me."

"That is ... what I ... believe," Mina whispered, "and it is very, very wonderful ... but supposing when we are ... married you grow ... tired of me ... as you have ..."

Before she could say any more, the Marquis had put his fingers against her lips.

"I know what you are thinking," he said, "and it is something you are forbidden to say or to think again. You are as well aware as I am, Mina, that what we feel for each other is utterly different from anything that has ever happened to me in the past. And if there have been women of whom you disapprove in my life before we met, it is your fault for being so long in coming to me!"

Mina gave a little laugh.

"You cannot really ... blame me for ... that."

"I blame no-one but myself. But you must not think of me disapprovingly. All that matters is that we have found each other. We are together and our lives now start anew. Because I have been so fortunate, mine will be very, very different from what it has been in the past."

His lips moved over the softness of her skin as he said:

"Everything about you not only excites but thrills and stimulates me to a new kind of thinking which will revolutionise my whole way of life. There are a great number of new and important things for us to do together."

"That is what I ... want ... not only to love you ... but also to ... help you."

"Which you have done already," the Marquis answered. "You have opened new doors in my mind, just as you have opened others I have not thought of in years. But, my darling, this is only the beginning."

She moved a little closer and, lifting her face, said:

"I ... love you! I love ... you! How can you say all the things I want to hear and make me feel that I am not too young, or poor or unimportant, but somebody ... worthy of your ... love?"

"I will make you sure of your importance as soon as we are married," the Marquis said, "and I do not intend to wait one moment longer than is necessary to get a Special Licence."

As if the words gave him an urgency to start immediately, he rose to his feet and pulled Mina to hers.

Then he put his arm round her and stood for a moment looking over the fens towards the sea.

"Now I understand so much that puzzled me about you before," he said. "Living here, how could you not be one with all the winged creatures that come when you call them, just as you called me with your magic, from which there was no escape."

Mina smiled.

"Just as the birds have a strange, infallible instinct for where they belong," she said softly, "I knew the moment I saw Vent Royal and then you that that was where I belong. Deep down in my heart, I knew that I had come home, and my brain accepted it later."

"You must always follow your heart, my precious one," the Marquis said with a smile.

"That is not difficult... because now... it is ... yours," Mina whispered.

She looked so lovely as she said it that he kissed her again, his lips holding her captive possessively, until once again a rising flame united them and the fire of it seemed to be part of the sunshine.

Then the Marquis released Mina to take her by the hand.

"Come, my precious one," he said. "We are going home! Home to a place of love which you will fill with your own special magic from which neither of us can ever escape."

For a moment they looked into each other's eyes.

Then in the glory of the sunshine they ran hand-in-hand through the flower-filled grass, enveloped by the irresistible magic that is true love.

ABOUT THE AUTHOR

Barbara Cartland, the world's most famous romantic novelist, who is also an historian, playwright, lecturer, political speaker and television personality, has now written over 300 books.

She has also had many historical works published and has written four autobiographies as well as the biographies of her mother and that of her brother Ronald Cartland, who was the first Member of Parliament to be killed in W. W. II. This book has a preface by Sir Winston Churchill and has just been republished with an introduction by Sir Arthur Bryant.

Barbara Cartland has sold 200 million books over the world, more than half of these in the U.S.A. She broke the world record in 1975 by writing twenty-three books and the four subsequent years with 20, 21, 23 and 24. In addition her album of love songs has just been published, sung with the Royal Philharmonic Orchestra.

Barbara Cartland, who is a Dame of the Order of St. John of Jerusalem has championed the cause for old people and founded the first Romany Gypsy Camp in the world.

Barbara Cartland is deeply interested in Vitamin Therapy and is President of the British National Association for Health. Her book the *Magic of Honey* has sold in millions all over the world.

She has a magazine *The World of Romance* and her Barbara Cartland Romantic World Tours will, in conjunction with British Airways, carry travelers to England, Egypt, India, France, Germany and Turkey.